Naga
Invasion

Jack Enright

DEDICATION

For the love of Tatiana

CONTENTS

ACKNOWLEDGMENTS

I would like to thank Adele Brinkley for her patience in editing the manuscript. Also I thank the Museo del Prado for featuring the work of Giovanni Battista Tiepoli, the source of the book cover.

i

INVASION OF PORTLAND

"Launch the Dragon ships! Invade every city, rape, pillage and plunder! Here are special orders for you my trusted one. Fire on La Palma in the Canary Islands until the mountain splits and falls into the sea. The Prophecy must be fulfilled!" Lord Tolpiltzin bellowed.

"Consider it done my Lord." Attalus calls out in reply. "Poseidon will give us ultimate victory!"

"The United States of America will be sorry they joined with the Nishi." Tolpiltzin blustered with a wry smile. "I will stay with my ship until you return in victory to rescue the elite."

"All pilots launch your vessels!" Attalus yelled to the crew. "We attack Oceanus!"

Tolpiltzin saw the Nishi flagship approaching to board his damaged vessel, the flagship of the Nagas. He quickly decided to bail and escaped on a Dragon ship, leaving elite Nagas and crew to fend for themselves. Enroute he broadcasted a message to the people of Oceanus by way of their satellite.

"People of Oceanus, hear my words. I am Tolpiltzin, leader of the Naga warriors. We have come to Oceanus to renew our bond with our kin from ages past. We once lived here in the dawn of civilization. We have returned to show the people of Oceanus a new way of life for all. We welcome all people who would join us in our quest for knowledge and discovery. You can partake of the discovery of other worlds in distant star systems. In the days of yore, our ancestors honored the true gods of space and time. For their loyalty they were awarded passage on starships to the home of the gods. On our planet the gods have taught us to construct universities and become teachers in science and technology.

"As Admiral of the Naga Galactic Fleet, I am prepared to offer scholarships and free passage to worthy candidates. However at this hour we have entered into a unexpected conflict with a race of aliens not of this world. These strange extraterrestrials intend to deny us entry into our ancestral home Oceanus. We ask your help in fighting the Nishi an alien race. We K'ny who have returned are human like you. You are our brothers and sisters. We are family. We seek refuge here now that the Nishi have attacked us in space."

Spoon and Judy watched the Nishi starship carrying their friends launch from Riverfront Park in Portland and head into the sky until it vanished over Mt Hood. It was a clear day and they caught the Light Rail to Mount Tabor. All their friends were gone far away to another world 400 light years away but they had decided to stay on Oceanus and make a life together. They hoped the Nishi would stay and help to defeat the Nagas.

Sergeant Witherspoon and Private Judy Ishimaru of the National Guard heard the news of the

Naga defeat by the combined fleets of the USA, China, Japan and India. Now Russia, Korea and the Philippines had joined the coalition to fight the Naga invasion of Kamchatka. There were rumors of a Dragon ship siting over Seattle. Spoon wanted to travel east to fight against the Nagas and to contact his folks in South Carolina. Judy consented to go with him. Her folks had left on a Nishi starship departing from Seattle. Months ago they fled the East coast because of the terrible onslaught of the Tsunami and the loss of so many friends and neighbors. There was inconsolable sadness in their hearts and eyes of people they met and also a mounting rage against the Naga.

At the top of Mt. Tabor, Spoon and Judy watched the sun set over the Ocean. A peaceful twilight descended over the metropolis. Judy prepared fish for dinner as Spoon tended the fireplace. A rumble and loud noise rocked the house. Spoon went outside and saw an explosion north near the airport.

"This must be a Naga invasion," remarked Spoon in a tone of bewilderment.

"I suppose I was naïve in thinking the Naga were defeated and would leave our planet," Judy replied, her lips trembling in shock.

Despondent, Spoon said, "It won't be long before they find us here and bomb our home."

"You are not giving up on me now, are you, big boy?" Judy nudged him with a smile.

"Anger has taken hold of me. I was hoping to have a good time tonight. We cannot stay here and live in peace."

"Let's make use of that anger and kick their ass!" exclaimed Judy.

"Looks like they are headed this way in a hurry!" declared Spoon.

Judy agreed. "We had better leave."

They decided to leave but not by train because the electricity may have been cut off.

"Koko left a rocket propelled hover craft in the garage," Judy uttered.

"He is one handy fella. You know how to drive it?" Spoon asked doubtfully.

"Yup, Koko showed me how, and took me around the hills here."

"All right let's get it fired up," Spoon replied with gusto.

Judy fired up the craft, and Spoon jumped in and they headed toward downtown Portland.

Spoon was suddenly alarmed. "You are taking us toward the danger zone."

"Yes, we have no weapons." Judy grinned mischievously. "I know where there is a stash at a Pizzeria."

"What will you do if we encounter a Dragon ship?" Spoon asked.

"Put on this armor. It's made of fullerene and will shield your body from their blasters." Judy spoke in a maternal tone with a twist of irony.

"How about you?" Spoon replied.

"Get me a suit as well, darling. They are stored in the back." Judy replied affectionately.

They soon arrived at the Pizzeria near the plaza downtown. Together they had pizza and juice but they could hear explosions to the west, they getting closer by the minute. Judy went to the back of the restaurant to find the stash of weapons.

An explosion rocked the block destroying the restaurant. Judy was protected behind a concrete wall behind the building. She got up trying to shake off the initial shock and stumbled into the rubble to look for Spoon. She called out for Spoon in the desolation and dug through the rubble hoping to find him alive. She heard commotion outside and saw troops of Naga warriors approaching. She ran to the rear of the ruins behind the wall to the hover craft. Holding back the tears she vowed to avenge Spoon and face the Nagas in battle. She fired up the craft, activated the protective shield and blasted out of there. The sky was dark but the city was lit up in flames amid the smoke of burning buildings. Soon she saw two stragglers along the road. One was dressed in Nishi armor. Stopping to get a closer look she recognized a friend she thought had taken flight.

"Brian, is that you? I thought you took to the stars, spaceman?" Judy exclaimed.

"Hey Judy, what a nice surprise it is to see you. It's me all right. The Nishis had other plans for me." Brian replied.

"And who is this fellow, may I ask?" Judy asked.

"You may my lady. I am Ulani of the Nishi," he replied nobly.

"Welcome aboard friends," Judy declared. Ulani, perhaps you can tell me how to find friendly forces?"

"You are looking at it." Ulani joked.

"So you two are going to take on the Naga fleet, I suppose?" Judy suppressed a laugh.

"With a little help from our friends, we will seize the day." Ulani spoke in a confident manner but this time with a British accent.

"Ok, enough of the fun and games guys. Just tell me where our troops are." Judy was exasperated.

"Yes, just head southeast toward Gresham. We have a secure base there," Ulani disclosed.

"Ulani, how do you come to know English so well?" Judy asked.

"What you never heard of Star Trek?" Ulani joked with a wide grin.

"Oh so I suppose people who live in faraway galaxies grow up learning proper English," Judy laughed to hear about her favorite show. "Yet if we go south of the border I will need a translator."

Ulani conceded he was cornered. "Ok you got me there. I lived here for some time in San Diego. I was stationed at the Naval Base in coordination with a treaty of cooperation between the USA and the Nishi."

Judy laughed. "I've got to admit you have a sense of humor. So Brian what made you stay here? Is your family still here?"

"I am working on a project to build a spaceship. My family is still here in Portland and I need to get to them soon," Brian replied stoically.

"You can drop off Brian. His home is along the way," Ulani remarked.

"Do you have a pen somewhere?" Brian asked Judy.

"Look in the compartment in front there," Judy said.

Brian opened the compartment and noticed an envelope. There he saw an envelope with 'SECRET' stamped on it.

"Ulani, I believe this envelope is best kept in your hands. It's addressed to Admiral Mitsuo," Brian remarked with uncharacteristic urgency.

"Koko must have left that here. He must have forgotten about it," Judy speculated.

"You never know about Koko. The letter could be his idea of a joke," Ulani suggested.

Brian inquired. "Judy, how is your friend Spoon?"

She hesitated before she answered. "He was lost in the bombing of a Pizzeria we were visiting tonight." Her speech faltered on her trembling lips. "I don't know if he is still alive, I had to leave because the Nagas arrived on the scene." She could no longer hold back tears and wept.

"You should have told us sooner. Maybe we could have radioed for help," Brian consoled.

Judy recovered when she thought of the wicked Nagas. She sought revenge.

Ulani offered to help. "That's ok Judy. We will send a force to look for him but first drop off Brian. His place is nearby."

Judy dropped Brian off in a residential area, miles from the combat zone. A few minutes later, she and Ulami arrived at the base where she dropped off Ulani.

"Thanks for the ride. Where will you go from here?" Ulani asked.

"To attack the Nagas and avenge Spoon," Judy asserted her will to fight on.

She saw a strange sight in the sky to the Northwest. Maybe it was an eagle or a vulture but the shape looked more like something prehistoric.

"Do you see that flying over there?" Judy cried out in alarm.

"That is a Naga dragon. A Naga commander is here and has unleashed his pets," Ulani spoke plainly.

"A Dragon...you mean a fire breathing Dragon?" Judy asked incredulously.

"Yes. Terror is loosed upon your people," Ulani said to awaken her inmost being.

"I am going to smoke that dragon," Judy cried out in anguish and rage.

Never before had she the desire to fight. She longed for peace and tranquility, but now a raging violence without end descended upon her. Something inside her changed and transformed her as an avenging angel. Not a fire or flame but coolness of spirit calmed her mind and filled her with light.

"Judy, I have a few words to say to you before I leave on this urgent mission to secure these plans," Ulani put his hand on her shoulder. "You are of the Nephali of Oceanus, a beloved sister of the Nishi. I bless you on this mission to avenge Oceanus. May Amaterasu bless you."

"Thank you Ulani. My mother told me I would one day fight against evil in a battle. That day is now before me." Judy's eyes shined with a beauteous light.

"Be sure to wear the helmet to protect you from the scorching fire. Wherever you go you will soon find allies. I must go now." Ulani hugged her and bid her Au revoir.

"Goodbye Ulani." Judy whispered as he left on his journey.

Judy drove northwest toward the Rose City Cemetery. Ulani's words filled her with hope and she wondered how she came to be a Nishi warrior. To defend Oceanus was her destiny.

As she arrived on North Fremont Street Judy saw soldiers battling Naga Storm troopers surrounding Beaumont Middle School. She parked the hover craft and assessed the scene. A dragon with a rider on its back was gliding over the school. Judy put on her helmet and grabbed a blaster. A blast of fire spewed from the mouth of the dragon toward the soldiers who took refuge behind parked cars and ran for shelter as the Storm troopers advanced on the school. Judy fired at the dragon. Hit in the neck, the dragon fell to earth, its rider landed on the roof of the school. She ran to where the dragon fell and stood over it. She pulled a sword from a scabbard on her side and severed its head... her first kill.

Judy advanced toward the Naga Storm troopers who now were targeting her with fire. Thankfully, her suit protected her from the cosmic ray blasters. She suddenly felt a surge of energy and took off in a burst of speed toward the foe eluding their shots. As she approached the first Naga, he reached for a hammer from his side to strike her knowing she was vulnerable to blunt force. She cut off his arm before he could lift it and cut him down. She moved through the Naga pack, faster than lightning. To her they were moving in slow motion. She charged through enemy lines scorching the foe with bursts of lasers and setting them to flames and ashes. A blue light surrounded her for she carried a sword of lightning.

Soldiers of the Guard welcomed her arrival.

"Whoever you are, we are glad to see you blessed lady!" Private Tom spoke with astonishment.

"I am Judy of the Nishi here to protect you from the Naga."

"Well young lady you are doing a good job. We are behind you. Lead us the way to vanquish the foe," Major Mike replied enthusiastically.

The soldiers were equipped with sufficient body armor and weaponry to take on the storm troopers but they were no match for fire breathing Dragons. However they did have radio communication and fire support. Major Mike Mc Quire contacted Guard base for air support. Commander of base sent a pilot on a mission with an A-10 warthog to hunt down the dragons harassing the troops.

Lieutenant Will Powers climbed into the cockpit, did his preflight check and got clearance for takeoff from ground personnel. His blood was hot ready to blast a Dragon ship to smithereens. Nishi had provided the Guard with fullerene armor to protect the airframes and personnel from cosmic ray blasters.

Naga storm troopers were burning a swath from the airport through Portland and heading toward high points, at Mt. Tabor and Powell Butte. Looting was already occurring by turncoats who allied with the Naga for leftovers. Martial law was declared and the order was to shoot on sight for any looters caught red handed.

But there was yet another trick Commander Juba of the Naga unleashed on the people of Portland. Juba would sniff out any people hiding out with his voracious reptilian pets.

With the help of Judy, the Guard eliminated the Naga troops surrounding the school and set up a perimeter to safe guard the people sheltered inside from the ongoing battle.

Brian was a NASA scientist presently a guest lecturer in Quantum Physics at PSU. He and his family were witnessing the Naga invasion in their neighborhood in east Portland. In their basement hidden and from view they saw scenes of destruction and gore. Brian's daughter Emily pointed to refugees surrendering to Naga commands and offering food. Brian and his wife Alicia were shocked at what they saw. Bodies of adult men and women were strapped on poles crucified. They witnessed beatings, whippings and beheadings from a shielded window in their underground home. The K'ny mercenaries were indeed ruthless and cruel. But at least they did not cut the hearts out of living people like the Aztecs did.

Now Brian and Alicia wished they had taken the Nishi transport out of Portland. They had heard of a Nishi starship that was engaging the enemy nearby, so there was hope. Emily looked out the window and turned around white with fear.

"What is it, Emily?" Alicia alarmed at the sight of her daughter stricken with horror.

Emily was frozen, unable to speak. Brian went over to Emily and held her. He looked out and saw a strange creature eight feet tall with a red crest of feathers atop his head, very long wide nose, deep set large eyes, long gangly legs and arms and six fingers on each hand. The head looked curious, sloped forehead with enlarged cerebellum. Only thirty feet away from the window, the creature looked around accompanied by feathery reptilians with jaws full of teeth. They sniffed about on all fours and stood in front of the window.

"Alicia, we have been discovered. We must leave at once," Brian whispered in alarm.

Alicia grabbed backpacks of supplies prepared earlier, giving one to Brian as they made their escape into a tunnel. Brian had made a tunnel nearly a hundred feet long into a wooded area. Hurriedly they made their escape.

Judy jumped into the hover craft with the Private Tom of the Guard. He would provide her with updates on the position of Naga troop movements. She saw what looked like large chickens with colorful feathers. They were slashing at dogs that were chasing them. Soldiers moved in and shot the creatures down. Judy arrived at the top of Mt. Tabor and parked to get a good view of the scene below.

From her vantage point she looked northwest and saw the path of destruction left by the Nagas, burning and demolished neighborhoods. Out of the smoke rising from the city she saw a few dragon riders in the sky in the distance. Then she noticed a Navy jet take out one of the dragon riders, the rider falling to his death as the dragon fell to earth. She recognized the aircraft. It was an A-10 warthog. Suddenly a Dragon ship 300 feet long appeared and attacked the A-10 with a burst of purple against its airframe but it was deflected off the fullerene armor. Pilot Will Powers shot a ten second burst of depleted uranium shells into the Dragon ship riddling it from stem to stern. Lights went out in the ship as it swayed and plummeted to earth.

Judy rushed back to the hover craft to capture survivors of the wreck.

"Tom, let's go!" Judy shouted. "We are going to board that Dragon ship."

"Should we abandon our position?" Tom was hesitant to assault a Dragon ship.

"Our priority now is to capture the Naga commander and crew." Judy spoke with confidence.

Impressed with her valor, Tom replied. "Yes. I will alert the troops to go to that position."

"Here are the coordinates." Judy pointed to a GPS tracker on the dash of the hover craft.

Judy arrived at the base of the butte where the Dragon ship crashed. Guard troops were already assembled and surrounding the vessel when a door opened at the port side by the prow. Judy shot a blast near the door. Naga troops limped out with their hands up as the Guard soldiers held guns ready to fire. One tall Naga in a black robe had a hood over its head. Judy was instantly suspicious of him.

"Tom, tell the soldiers to single that black robe out," Judy commanded.

Soldiers took hold of the Naga and pulled back the hood. A crest of red on a strange looking head emerged. It was the Naga commander, Juba. His head fell forward and then he wrestled to get a knife from his side. A soldier shot him with a tazer and he fell to the ground. He was bound and captured. Being captured by humans was a tremendous disgrace for the Naga. He was going to commit suicide rather than being taken alive by inferior humans.

A party of rescuers dug through the rubble and found Spoon still alive and breathing. He was badly bruised and had sustained a broken arm, ribs and leg. He was taken to the hospital in the southeast of town. Recovering he asked for Judy but was told only a few survived the blast in the area and she was not among them.

Spoon was heartbroken and wondered why the loss of his dear friend Judy had become his fate. But news of the victory against the Nagas cheered him up despite the wholesale destruction of one third of the populous city. Two Dragon ships and ten transports were destroyed, and ten thousand Nagas captured or killed. Naga Commander Juba was captured and detained in maximum security. He was found to be guilty of killing two pilots in an earlier incident on the border of Arizona and Mexico. Now he was held for the invasion of Portland. The Naga Storm troopers also known as the K'ny were found to be human through DNA analysis with markers of J haploid. Koko's story of their migration to a distant planet in the Pleiades star system was confirmed in interrogation with Nishi interpreters. Not all Naga warriors were as clever as Lord Tolpiltzin. Spoon heard about a heroine who singlehandedly destroyed a Naga transport and vanquished nine hundred warriors. She was said to be invisible, moving as quickly as lightning, and when standing with a sword in hand she shined in a blue light.

HEART OF THE SCORPION

Will Powers woke up on a clear sunny day on the outskirts of Brunswick. He brushed his teeth and took his Chiweenie for a walk in Elmwood Cemetery. Gazing at the clouds he saw a UFO coming closer from behind the patchy clouds to the south. The UFO appeared to be a large aircraft accelerating but then he saw two other fighter jets chasing it. As the UFO approached nearly overhead it dove near treetop level. Wow, it was the size of an aircraft carrier, and soon it passed over the city with the two jets pursuing at higher altitude. He hurried back to tell his girlfriend the exciting news.

"Tatiana, you won't believe what I saw!" Will exclaimed.

"I saw it too from the balcony. What could those ships be? Tatiana replied, her green eyes staring at the sky.

"I guess it could have been a Naga ship chased by jet aircraft," Will suggested with mirth.

"Are the stories true? Have we been invaded by aliens from another world?" I'm scared Will," Tatiana stammered.

Will held Tatiana in his arms to comfort her. "I am not really sure what to believe but I don't think we have aircraft that size. It must be an alien ship, so I suppose it could be true. Let's hope I am wrong or we may be facing the same threat as Portland."

Tatiana put aside her fear for a moment. "Come inside, I will fix your favorite oatmeal mix for breakfast."

A few moments later, she placed two steaming bowls of oatmeal with sunflower seeds, raisins and carob on the table. The two looked out the window facing the street in expectation of what might invade the skies above their home. Tatiana slowly poured coconut milk into each bowl. Will savored the meal with each spoonful.

"I would like to spend the day with you, my love, but I have to go to the University to attend lectures," Will looked into her eyes with affection.

Disappointed Tatiana said. "And you genius now better hop off to your studies before you are late again."

She gave him a hug and kiss. He reveled in her embrace feeling the fire down below. She pushed him away and giggled. He swung the backdoor open waved to his love and jumped in his classic Mini Cooper.

Driving down Livingston Avenue, Will noticed many people looking up to the sky, pointing and talking. Apparently they had seen the UFO as well. He was aware Tatiana was not handling the situation very well. Just a few months ago an X Class Solar Flare disrupted the Northeast leaving the town in darkness and chaos. Operations were back to normal but the atmosphere downtown was subdued as if a dark cloud hung over the town. Strange personages appeared, walking about town and attracting crowds.

Tatiana spoke to Will later in the day about an odd encounter after work.

"I noticed strange people strolling about town today and I met a strange dude at the Natural Food store after work," Tatiana said uneasily.

Will chuckled. "Did he ask for your number?"

"No not the usual line. He invited me to come to a meeting and to bring a friend. He was talking to Belinda about a demonstration at Rutgers campus." Tatiana replied, puzzled by the incident.

"What did he look like?"

"He was about your size but he had pointed ears, a distinct aquiline nose and blazing aquamarine eyes. He was very polite and curious, had a deep tan and talked in a strange accent kind of like a surfer... said his name was Koko," Tatiana replied.

"I have heard of this guy from talk on campus. Some say he has very interesting talks but some say he is a kook," Will remarked casually.

"Kook or not he bought some ginseng and Belinda likes him. So are you going to the meeting with me? It's at the Cook campus by Passion Puddle tomorrow afternoon."

"All right I've got Saturday off. I would like a stroll and meet some friends," Will replied with his characteristic nonchalance.

Leaves were falling on a breezy autumn day in Brunswick, as Will and Tatiana drive over to Cook campus to join the rally.

Will was curious. "So what do you think this rally is all about?"

"Belinda told me Koko is going to talk about the UFO we saw yesterday."

"Maybe he was the dude with pointed ears piloting the craft." Will wryly joked with her.

"That would be interesting."

Will parked in the street and they walked across to the campus.

"Hey, Rory, it's good to see you!" Will yelled to his friend.

Rory came up to see his friends. "Will, Tatiana so you have come to hear Koko speak?" Rory came up to see his friends.

"Yea, Tatiana met him yesterday. Gee I'm surprised to see such a large crowd." Will remarked.

"He's a really popular dude around here. He is a world class surfer from California." Rory explained.

"So, this is about surfing?" Will asked suspiciously.

"Not really, he is here to talk about a distant planet Tengoku." Rory

"So he is an alien like I surmised from Tatiana's description." Will inferred. "The Japanese know Tengoku as the kingdom of heaven."

"Yes, I have heard this from Koko." Rory affirmed.

"So, this dude is a kook." Will concluded coolly.

"Just listen and decide for yourself. He is about to speak." Rory replied smiling buoyantly.

Will thought about the time ten years ago when he first visited Rutgers as a freshman. He met a girl the first semester and together they sat beneath the willow by the pond. She kissed him sweetly as a breeze rippled across the pond. At his fraternity down the road, upperclassmen invited him into poker games and spiked the lemonade with 100 proof ethyl alcohol. Losing at poker was not so bad but the alcohol took its toll quickly. He fell to drinking beer, wine or whisky every night, dating girls, missing classes and losing track of his studies entirely. It took him five years to recover but now he was back all the wiser. At least, Will believed so.

"Fair is my love but

Not so fair as fiddle

Mild as a dove but

Neither true nor trusty." Will Shakespeare

Will woke from his revelry as Koko began to speak:

"I called many of you here because you saw a strange ship flying over your town. How many of you here saw this ship?"

A few held up their hands, and then others joined in until nearly all were raised.

"Don't be afraid! Be of good courage. A Nishi starship is stationed nearby to protect your city! " Koko exclaimed.

"Who are the Nishi?" people in the crowd murmured

"I am of the Nishi! We have come to protect you from ruthless cunning invaders who have attacked Oceanus!" Koko shouted in a booming voice.

"We have heard of these invaders!" people in crowd shouted.

"Yes they are intergalactic pirates known as the Nagas," Koko called out to them.

"So, this is an invasion force from outer space?" a newscaster inquired of Koko.

"Yes indeed it is. You have been kept in the dark. The invasion has been going on for weeks on the West Coast and across the globe. Therefore, I advise you to listen and obey instructions by the National Guard. Officers please come forth now." Koko beckoned.

Colonel Mackenzie, Lieutenant Jameson, Captain Armstrong and Sargent Witherspoon strode to the front to stand with Koko. Colonel Mackenzie addressed the crowd:

"Rest assured people, Koko speaks the truth. Sargent Spoon Witherspoon has just returned from the Battle of Portland. He was nearly killed by a Naga blast and buried in a pile of rubble. He is here today to tell his story."

Sargent Witherspoon stepped forward to speak. He was interrupted by a wave of applause and cheers from the crowd. When they quieted, he spoke into the microphone to address the crowd.

"So many people have died at the bloody hands of the Nagas but I am alive and wonder why I was saved. I live to fight another day against this relentless and savage attack on our people, on Oceanus! I know Koko personally as a friend of mine. I can assure you that he is a friend of the people of Oceanus, to all of us together who share this wonderful planet. It was Koko and a band of soldiers who rescued me from the rubble of a blast in downtown Portland. It was there that I lost my dear loved one Judy. I fear the Nagas killed her. We must all stand together and not listen to the wiles of the Nagas. It is incomprehensible how they have come this far to rape, pillage and plunder our homes. We had better wake up and change our ways so we deserve to live here on Oceanus."

Captain Armstrong stepped up to speak.

"Thank you Sargent Witherspoon for your words of encouragement. We are proud members of the National Guard here to protect the people from this menace. Together with the Nishi, we beat them in Portland and if we stand together we can beat them here. It is indeed true that the Nishi are a race of people from a distant star system the Pleiades but they

20

are allied with our government to give whatever help we need in this time of trouble."

A cry was heard in the crowd. "Spoon!" A woman called and ran to the front through the crowd. "Spoon. I am here!"

Will drifted away from the crowd. All this talk of a Naga invasion disturbed him. Tatiana looked about, and not seeing Will, she walked toward Lyman Hall. She found Will walking along the road. Puzzled she called out to him.

"Hey, Will, where are you going?"

Will turned to look at the blond beauty with green eyes. He looked at her amazed that she might care about him. He wanted to get away from the crowd.

"Are you running out on me?" Tatiana scolded him.

Will relented and turned back toward her. Tatiana grabbed him and smiled.

"Sometimes I wonder what going on inside your head dreamer." She shook her head.

"Hey, Tatiana, come on over here girl!" A lady with long black hair and blue eyes appeared. It was Belinda from the store with a few friends whom Tatiana knew as classmates at Rutgers a few years back.

"Will, I will be with my friends for a little while." Tatiana said cheerfully.

"Ok I'll just hang here with Rory" Will replied.

Will saw his nemesis Valentin climbing up the hill, and watched him stroll through the crowd toward Tatiana. He had not seen Valentin in the past year. Tatiana had been his girlfriend before he went overseas. Tatiana's eyes met Valentin's gaze and she spoke to him in her native Russian.

"Nice to see you, Valentin."

"You look wonderful my dear."

Will thought about going to intervene but it was no use. Tatiana's dalliance with Valentin would have to run its course. He sauntered out of the crowd and made his way home, disheartened by this reuion of the former lovers. His Master's thesis in meteorology the day before went well but now he was worried he would lose his girlfriend and his life would unravel. He decided to have a beer and later stopped over at Rory's.

"Hey, buddy, come on in." Rory welcomed his friend.

Will wasn't his usual easygoing self. "I'm a bit shaky today," Will said and told Rory of Tatiana and Valentin.

"She'll come back, you'll see." Rory reassured his friend.

Will remarked halfheartedly. "I hope you're right. She's a great gal."

"Hey, relax and have a seat. The Lions are playing the Cowboys."

"All right, the Lions are leading the Cowboys 7 to 0 in the first quarter," Will was excited.

"Great, I'll bring us some beers outta the fridge," Rory went out the kitchen.

"Someone's knockin at the door," Will said to Rory and went to answer the door.

"Hey, babe, brought you a friend." Tatiana hugged Will.

"Brian, I haven't seen you in a while. How you been?" Will gave his friend a hug.

"Hey Brian, how's NASA going for you?" Rory inquired.

"We're building a spaceship to go to the stars dude." Brian said proudly.

"That's got to be awesome dude." Rory exclaimed.

"You bet. It's interstellar dude." Brian.

"Who is the designer?" Will inquired.

"Some guy named Phineas, a real genius. We technicians don't see him much. It's got a magneto like a cyclotron around the shell of an ion propulsion rocket." Brian returned to his usual stoic manner of speaking.

"Ok genius, the Cowboys just tied the game with a touchdown." Tatiana attempted to change the subject.

"Grab a beer. It's microbrew here in Brunswick." Rory said.

Will whispered to Tatiana. "Say what was that dude Koko talking about?"

"I have it here on my phone. You can listen to it later. Just relax and enjoy the game babe." Tatiana whispered into his ear.

Will was eager now to hear the news, but when Tatiana cozied up to him, he relaxed on the couch resting his head on her milky white breasts. He had a lingering feeling of loss, a pang of heartbreak about to surface, but when she kissed him the darkness subsided for now.

The next day Will was invited to Brian's apartment across town. Brian was now a guest lecturer in Physics at Rutgers. Tatiana accompanied Will to dinner. She wanted to meet Brian's family.

"Will, how do I look in this blouse?" Tatiana demanded his attention.

"You look fine." Will replied with aplomb, admiring her legs.

"Oh you're no help. You always say that. Will, put on your blue herringbone jacket and a tie." Tatiana demanded. She was flustered with his coolness.

"You know I hate ties, but I'll put one on Sinatra style." Will egged her on for fun.

"You're impossible just wear a bowtie." Tatiana insisted.

"All right honey." Will gave up trying to humor her.

Will drove Tatiana across town to Brian's home, where he knocked on the door of the modest Cape Cod home. Brian had a surprise for Will as he entered his friend's home.

"Will, I'd like you to meet a friend of mine, Phineas." Brian introduced him to the distinguished spaceship designer.

Phineas got up and shook Will's hand.

"I hear you are a budding meteorologist." Phineas said with alacrity.

"I hope to earn my master's degree soon." Will replied.

Brian interjected. "Any snow in the forecast? I want to go skiing before the Nagas blow up the slopes."

Will's eyes lit up and he said. "Actually, I predict a blizzard within a week. Shiveluch has erupted on the Kamchatka peninsula sending a plume twelve kilometers into the stratosphere."

"What does that have to do with Northeast weather?" Brian replied.

"A volcanic plume of that mass and energy will divert the polar Jetstream above the Bering Strait and cause it to go from zonal to meridional, wavier thus generating a cyclone over the Northeast." Will asserted.

Phineas suggested. "You should write a paper on this theory and send it to the American Geophysical Society."

"I'm working on it, there is a lot of data to collect and analyze. Brian told me about your rocket design. " Will changed the subject.

"It's a team effort... many people are involved in the project." Phineas replied tactfully.

Will pried. "Could you tell me about it before dinner?"

"What do you want to know? Much of it is classified." Phineas feigned suspicion.

"Just the basic mechanics on how it works." Will stated plainly.

Phineas tested his knowledge. "Are you familiar with the ion propulsion engine?"

"Yes, is that all there is to it?" Will expected something new.

Phineas gave him more ideas to chew on. "No, we added a whole new dimension to it. It's called a resonance electron cyclotron rocket or magneto plasma rocket."

"That's a mouthful. What's the maximum velocity you expect from this rocket?" Will was now hooked.

Phineas replied. "Presently we approximate one tenth light speed but the upper limit is light speed."

"Are you familiar with the sun's magnetic field propagation of light, thus the limitation of light speed in the heliosphere?" Brian added.

Will questioned this line of reasoning. "Are you saying particles can travel faster than light outside the heliosphere?"

"Research confirms that particles can travel forty to one hundred times faster beyond the heliosphere, the magnetic field being that much stronger." Brian contended.

"That is the focus of our project. We can tune the magnetic field of the rocket to resonate with the galactic magnetic field to exceed the speed of light as we perceive here on Oceanus." Phineas backed up his colleague Brian.

"How can you protect the shell of the rocket at such high velocities and heat?" Will challenged the idea of light speed travel.

"The rocket shell has vents that leak plasma and a magnetic field enclose a protective shield around the rocket." Phineas explained his rocket shell design.

Will wondered. "Won't the plasma melt the shell of the rocket?"

"The shell is composed of carbon fiber composite with tungsten and a carbon nanotube interior, which conducts electromagnetic energy. Aerogel is also used to insulate the shell from heat. Piezoelectric crystal sensors sense any perturbation to the skin." Phineas explained.

Will exclaimed. "Wow we are about to enter a new era!"

"There's more you should know." Brian encouraged him.

"Should we tell him?" Phineas teased.

Brian pretended not to know. "Tell him what?"

"Ok let him have it." Phineas set the hook.

"A new era has indeed begun. Twelve years ago we were officially contacted by visitors from another world." Brian gave Will the whole story.

Will was skeptical but curious. "You are joking right?"

"We brought you here at the request of the Feds. Are you in or out?" Brian gave Will the ultimatum.

"I'm in give me the scoop." Will figured he had nothing to lose.

Brian whispered. "Ok but you are responsible if a leak should come from your lips."

"Hatches secure. Loose lips sink ships." Phineas added with a nod.

Will vowed. "Aye, aye your secret is safe with me."

"Koko, the surfer dude, is our contact. He and his crew have been helping us develop technology to combat the looming menace." Brian confided to Will.

Will was suspicious of this newcomer Koko. "That certainly raises a few questions. Namely how has Koko been helping us?"

"They call themselves the Nishi. They have helped us to mass produce a unique substance, ultra-hard fullerene, which is three hundred times stronger than high carbon steel yet as flexible as clothing." Phineas stated frankly.

Will's curiosity was burning. "So, this is the material that is used to shield the rocket in transit?"

"Yes, not only the rocket but we are using it to shield our warships, tanks, armored vehicles, aircraft, and personnel." Phineas fed Will's thirst for knowledge.

Will was missing a piece of the puzzle. "Then that brings me to the second question. Who is this nemesis you speak of?"

"Nagas, they are a people from a faraway planet who have come to invade our world for resources." Brian replied.

"Boys, dinner is ready." Alicia broke her husband's chain of thought for a moment.

Brian warned Will. "You heard the lady. Not a word to the ladies about any of this story."

"Understood." Will pledged.

Brian reminded Will of his younger brother, reddish brown hair, bright brown eyes and a noble air about him. It was comforting to have him around, his quick wit was refreshing.

Curiosity about these Nagas and Nishis was burning in Will but he held his tongue.

Brian thought of a social movement that had faded and dropped out of the news but was now making a rebound. There had always been people who believed in a higher power, a connection with a cosmic consciousness. Then there were those who elevated themselves above all others with power and authority rightly belonging to the divine. Now an unknown force had revived this movement known as the Spirit of the Age, Zeitgeist.

Tatiana was helping her friend Belinda, who managed the Natural Food Store in downtown Brunswick.

Tatiana noticed a customer who might need assistance. "Hello how can I help you?"

A handsome tall dark man turns around.

"Valentin, what a surprise it is to see you!" Tatiana exclaimed.

"Thought I might find you here, I was looking for a green eyed lady." Valentin turned to look at her figure with mirth in his eyes.

Tatiana knew his debonair charm and would not fall for it now. "You've been away for a while. Things have changed."

Valentin proposed a cultural treat, something he knew she yearned for.

"I thought you might be interested in attending a meeting tonight at the old theatre."

"Oh, you mean old times with your socialist friends?" Tatiana replied.

"Nothing like that, I just want to be friends. Have you heard of the Z movement?" Valentin tempted her curiosity.

Tatiana thwarted his attempts to win her back. "Yes they purport to promote an ecological based economy. Sometimes I hear people talk about it at the accounting firm but it's just whispers in the wind to me."

"Actually, the movement has gained a lot of momentum and financial backing recently. It has the potential to dramatically change society." Valentin affirmed the movement's validity.

Tatiana was interested in financial matters. "So are you involved in this movement personally?"

"I have been for the past few years as a recruiting agent, which explains my travels." Valentin showed himself as a man of the world.

Tatiana was looking for a man financially secure. "I am intrigued. When does the meeting start?"

"At 5 p.m., It continues for hours with refreshments." Valentin saw the gleam in her eyes.

"Ok I will meet you there later." Tatiana agreed with a smile.

"Au revoir" Valentin spoke with a Russian accent.

Valentin, a photojournalist, had acquainted himself with wealthy influential people who had a market in off world trade... slaves, prostitutes, electronics, precious metals. He was gaining wealth by providing clandestine courier services between Nagas and merchants here. Now he had an opportunity to take a step up at work as a spy and trade secrets. That is where Paulina came in. Paulina, a Columbian lady, 5'2" with long black hair tan complexion studied geography at RU. Valentin thought he had found the right agent for the job. She was a temptress. If she fell for the Z movie then perhaps she could lure secrets from scientists.

Valentin had connections with Naga agents in a network leading to Naga Admiral Tolpiltzin. It was an immense operation involving the employment of established gangs of Oceanus to work in off world trade. Nagas were primarily interested in human slaves for breeding, working and lucrative enterprises especially in the trade of jewels and precious metals. Black market operations on the Oceanus side found it very profitable to trade with Nagas to procure funds for their prostitution rings, gambling dens, drug dealings and gun running.

Valentin pulled up outside the restaurant downtown where Paulina worked part time. Paulina was just leaving. She had an astonished look on her face.

"Valentin, is that your ride? I'm impressed!" Paulina exclaimed in a charming Columbian accent.

"Thank you, hop in." Valentin replied.

"My, oh my, are you wealthy now? This car is worth a fortune. It's a Lamborghini!" Paulina was overwhelmed.

"It was a gift from one of my esteemed clients." Valentin proudly replied.

"I thought you were a photojournalist. Now tell me what kind of business are you in?" Paulina suspicions were brewing.

Valentin told her that he was a bona fide businessman. "I assure you it's not smuggling. I run a courier business for rich entrepreneurs."

"That's amazing! I'm glad you are doing so well." Paulina was satisfied.

Valentin made himself out to be a socialist. "Now, Paulina listen to me. You never mind all this talk about wealth. We soon will be attending a seminar on the equitable distribution of wealth, sharing the planet's resources."

"Yes, I wouldn't mind you sharing some of that wealth with me darling." Paulina quipped.

Valentin laughed. "You're funny."

They arrived at the old theatre, the place was mobbed but they entered through the rear entrance, VIP only.

"Hello, Ralph. Can we have seats for me and the lady?" Valentin played the part of a gentleman.

"Certainly, Valentin, Yours are reserved up front." Ralph treated him like a respected VIP.

The movie began. It was the Z movie, 3pm show

"How did you like the movie?" Valentin asked Paulina after the movie.

Paulina declared compassionately. "I must say I'm captivated. Wish I could take part somehow. All those poor people starving, living in shacks while the rich do nothing to help."

"You can help but first let's talk to a few people here. There will be a meeting." Valentin suggested slyly.

Paulina joined the Z movement, and Valentin recruited her for a secret mission.

Valentin told her. "Nishi pirates have come to despoil the planet and wage war against the populace." She was under his spell.

Later in the afternoon Tatiana arrived at the theatre to meet with Valentin. She nearly balked at entering but went on. She saw Valentin in the front row. He waved her over, showing his confident smile. Tatiana smiled as she sat next to him. The Z movie began but she was not impressed with the implications of the film. She thought the leader of the movement pretentious and arrogant.

After the movie Valentin asked her: "How did you like it?"

"It was ok." Tatiana replied somewhat apathetically.

Valentin figured she was bored. "Not ready to join yet?"

"You know me, I don't join clubs." Tatiana spoke candidly.

"Good enough." Valentin replied.

They walked outside together.

"Would you like to go out with an old friend?" Valentin held out hope for another fling with her.

"Ok, Tonight is your lucky night." Tatiana suddenly gave in to his charms.

They walked together to their favorite restaurant. Later that night Tatiana stayed at Valentin's place. She told herself Will would be busy all night doing research. She slept for a few hours waking in the dark. She regretted not having left earlier. Now it hit her, the truth hurt down deep. She remembered all the bad things she said to Will and how she alienated him yet he remained faithful. Why she asked herself did she act this way? Will was handsome but he was not rich. She wanted to change him to suit her needs. For months she fought with him about his research calling it useless. She told him he was not a stable man. He could not afford to take her places she wanted to go. Will would often be gone on the weekends and sometimes for weeks. Then she started to call him derogatory names thinking he would "snap out of it." She even threatened to throw him out if he didn't look for a good paying job. But the past few weeks she relented a little and let him relax to complete his thesis. Yes she thought herself an independent woman. But where would that get her without a man like Will to love her? She looked into the darkness of night and saw she had made a decision that had cost her, the love of her life. Time would not turn back for her, and the tide was out.

Tatiana rushed out without waking Valentin to catch a bus back home. She arrived at home. It was still dark before dawn. She opened the door and tiptoed upstairs finding the house empty. She began to worry becoming frantic hating herself for being so careless. The life she knew with Will was starting to come apart. She realized she could have no real life with an adolescent playboy. Billy boy was gone, she feared lost to her lost...lost...lost. Oh what a loss and it was her fault for leaving. Snow was falling. Flakes danced on the window pane. She wished could be happy. Darkness was growing inside of her. Any hope of escaping the dark was gone. She cried in agony as the void crept in.

It was snowing in the streets of bustling Brunswick. Swirls of snowflakes drifted suddenly out of the darkness of space lit up by the streetlights. Will marveled at the flakes dazzling like sparks from the darkness. He recalled a forecast of a blizzard coming with the arctic express. It was peaceful walking on the brick paved street on his way to the University library.

Ideas swirled in his mind about volcanoes erupting on the Kamchatka peninsula across the Bering Sea. He took out his smartphone and checked the volcano discovery site...sure enough Shiveluch erupted a week ago sending a plume twelve kilometers into the stratosphere, more than enough to divert the jet stream. He would tell his friend Brian and get busy working on his theory of volcanic cyclogenesis. Thoughts of Tatiana, feelings of jealousy and suspicion arose in his mind about the past few days. He decided to put these thoughts aside and work for a purpose, to be positive. Later Will stopped at a tavern on the way home

"Hey, Billy boy!" Rory waved to Will

Will cheered up he strode over to his lively friend.

"Billy! Meet my friends Belinda and Helen." Rory had his arms around Belinda as her friend Helen beside her looked into Will's brown eyes.

Will looked Helen over...very nice features, a slim young lady, twenty something blond hair and blue eyes. Rory and Belinda were smiling at his admiration of Helen. Will was quiet and then spoke.

"How do you do?" Will said to Helen

"I'm fine. So you are Will Powers, the intrepid explorer, Rory told me about?" Helen replied.

Will joked. "That's me but I left my hat at home."

"I hear you are working on a fellowship." Helen returned.

"Yes in meteorology." Will replied looking into her blue eyes.

Rory ordered beer. "Billy! Drink up."

"So, what's the forecast, Mr. Weatherman?" Belinda asked.

"I believe we are in for a major storm." Will claimed.

Just then the sports news on the big screen was interrupted with a news flash. "Seattle is in ruins after the eruption of Mt. Rainer and invasion by the insidious Nagas." Belinda whispered to Helen, "Don't ask him about Tatiana."

"That's a real bummer. I hope those bastards don't come here and destroy our town." Rory blasted.

Will said to Rory. "It's only a matter of time. I've decided to stay and fight them to the end. I joined the Guard last month."

"I'm with you buddy, I joined a few days ago." Rory clinked glasses with his buddy.

Will laughed. "I never thought you would join the army, surfer dude."

"Hey man surfers are fighters. Don't take my wave dude." Rory gulped down his beer.

Belinda interrupted their male comradery. "Ok, boys, we girls are going to join up too."

"You mean to take us on in a drinking bout?" joked Rory.

Belinda stared at her man. "If you drink any more, we will have to carry you home."

Helen looked at her in consternation and then turned to look into Billy's eyes.

Rory finished his beer "Let's head over to my place friends. We can watch a game and forget about war for tonight."

"Sounds good to me." Billy was tired of chasing Tatiana. He put his arm around Helen and she liked it.

Together they all jumped into Rory's SUV and rolled down the road but Belinda was driving.

"Helen, do you go to school here?" Will wondered about this beauty.

"I graduated a few years ago, got a BS in oceanography." Helen stirred his curiosity.

"So, what do you think of this alien invasion?" Will liked the sound of her voice.

"Horrified, hope they don't land here. It seems like a page out of ancient history." Helen replied.

"What do you mean ancient history? Are you saying this has happened before?"

"5,000 years ago in India, the Mahabharata tells the story of the invasion of Asuras and their defeat at the hands of Lord Krishna." Helen offered a tidbit of Hindu legend.

"I thought that was just mythology." Will figured she was talking about religion.

"There are archaeological digs that uncovered the ruins of a nuclear holocaust. So myth or not it's happening now. The ancient gods have returned with a vengeance." Helen contended.

"You do mean the Nagas." Will did not think of the Nagas as gods.

"After the scenes of death and destruction on the West coast I'm convinced the Nagas are the same demons that invaded India thousands of years ago. However, I'm not sure of the Nishi." Helen spelled out her theory of alien invasion.

"I can introduce you to a Nishi warrior." Will figured he would trump her with the Big Kahuna.

"You know a Nishi? Wow I would like to meet one. Is it a male?" Helen was attracted to athletic men.

"Yes, he's a man or a male of a different species really. He is friendly, intelligent, well-spoken and knows our language." Will attempted to describe this strange personage he hardly knew.

"How did you get to know him?" Helen was keenly interested.

"A friend of mine introduced me to him. The Nishi are helping us to develop weapons and strategy against the Nagas." Will wanted to impress her.

"Wow, that reminds me of a song ...when you're down and out ...love is the answer. The Nishi must love us. I wonder why." Helen thought of the Nishi as liberators.

They arrived at Rory's place "I suppose they're angels like you." Will complemented her.

She laughed "You will introduce me to your friend, won't you, Will Powers? Helen nudged him, "...and the Nishi warrior."

"You can call me Billy." Will entrusted her with his nickname.

"Ok, Billy, now about this friend of yours. Are you going to introduce me?" Helen insisted.

"Sure, how about tomorrow?" Will suggested.

"Swell." Helen was content for now.

"Billy, you know there's a bed for you upstairs." Rory called out from the couch in the living room.

"Thanks Rory, I think I'll hit the sack. I'm tired." Will was trying to forget Tatiana.

"Sweet dreams, Billy." Belinda called cheerfully.

Billy went upstairs and fell into the bed, Helen followed him.

"Mind if I sleep next to you?" Helen asked.

"Please do. I need you to hold me." Will uttered.

She snuggled up to him.

Later he told her a secret.

Helen murmured. "There is an aura about you, Billy, like you are involved in some secret sort of plan, a mission bigger than academics."

"Ok, promise not to tell a soul what I am about to reveal to you." Will whispered.

"I promise with my heart and soul Billy." Helen vowed.

"I am a fighter pilot. We operate secretly since the beginning of this Naga offensive. When I get a call from base, I must respond immediately to perform my duty, to protect my people from danger." Will divulged to her.

"I understand Billy and admire you." Helen held him in her arms.

"So, you do understand the importance of secrecy?" Will asked.

"I do indeed for I also have been trained as a soldier." Helen said.

"That is wonderful to hear. We need brave women like you." Will kissed her.

Naga agents on Oceanus had other plans. Valentin's plan to steal secrets from the Nishi was about to enfold. On the outskirts of Brunswick, Valentin arrived at the Ramada Inn with Paulina. He escorted her into the hotel as the valet took the car. There was a convention of geophysical scientists meeting and Valentin had a special pass to attend. After the initial meetings they mingled with the guests at a dinner and Valentin singled one out to Paulina.

"Oh I want to meet him now." Paulina was eager.

Valentin held her back. "Not so soon darling, it's too early. Wait until he goes to the bar to have a drink."

Soon, Phineas went to the bar to have a whiskey and talked with a friend. Paulina walked over gracefully and sat close by admiring him. Phineas noticed her and moved to sit by her. After some small talk, Phineas and Paulina went to his room at the hotel. Phineas opened the door for his beautiful guest. He put his briefcase beside the sofa and offered to take her coat. She loosened the garment from her shoulder, placed her hand on his shoulder, and looked into his eyes. Her coat fell to the floor as they kissed passionately. He took her into the bedroom.

After a night of sex, Paulina found him sleeping and tiptoed into the living room. She found the briefcase. She looked through the bookcase and discovered schematics, diagrams and papers. She gathered the documents, quickly dressed, put the documents into her coat pocket and escaped out the door.

Outside she called Valentin who was waiting with the car. Her first mission accomplished' she imagined that she was in a James Bond movie. Valentin gave her an envelope with $10,000. Paulina was disappointed when Valentin dropped her off at her place and did not come upstairs with her. He said he was busy.

Valentin hurried out of town to a secret hideout in a Belle Mead farmhouse. He loved to take the drive and remembered his last time was with a Naga woman named Wangee. She was tall with muscular thighs and wide hips. He loved to massage her silky, iridescent skin and marveled over her exotic features. When she kissed him with her wide puffy lips, he was taken in completely. She held him tightly with her strong fingers six on each hand and let him suckle on her four breasts with exuberance. He put his fingers over her sloping forehead and ran them through her amarillo tuff of feathers that was her crest. Her waist was slender and taut with muscle as she thrust upon him with abandon. He held on to her protruding fleshy booty, and felt with intense desire as her clitoris gripped hold of him and bonded.

She was a hybrid of the Biru dynasty and yearned to have a child with Valentin. This time she hoped he would impregnate her for she was fertile when the moon was full. Even though she held him so tightly Valentin could not ejaculate until she released her grip. She held him for the ultimate pleasure until she felt he was totally bonded with her. Valentin fell into a dream state of bliss then burst forth upon her. She moaned and kissed him, shrieking with ecstasy and took him in again.

She laughed and told him she was Musrussu, a raging sea serpent. Knowing she came from the Red star in Scorpius, he called himself the stinger in her heart. She told him a secret known to few. Her guiding star was Kakkab Bir in the heart of the Scorpion. Her planet revolved around a smaller star in the constellation closer to Oceanus. The Riskani who had spent generations isolated from the Nishi held the mistaken belief that they were of the Pleiades like their ancestors.

She never told him the truth of her little star, but there was one who knew, and he was heading to the Gateway and knew of the secret passage to Tlalocan. He was a Riskani but also a spy for the Nishi. He followed a ribbon of strong magnetic force, forty times stronger than Helios, the star Oceanus revolves around. At 22 Light years from Oceanus, it would take him less than six months to reach his destination.

Beyond the Heliosphere, the galactic magnetic field of larger stars pulled starcraft toward their gravitational field at velocities that exceeded the speed of light within the Heliosphere. The scientists of Oceanus were on the verge of building spacecraft that could resonate with the galactic field and propel them toward distant galaxies. What lay in the darkness of Scorpius was a race of Pirates who had been drifting from their home planet for millennia. Their sun and its entire solar system were swallowed by a giant black hole known as Xibalba by the Mayan priests. It was the dark star and the nucleus of death that threatened Oceanus. It was these Lords of Death who roamed the cosmos, who first visited Tlalocan and brought the Nagas into their fold.

GATEWAY OF THE GALAXY

On the other side of town, Rory and his friends were stepping into a bar to have lunch. Rory called over a waitress and they ordered sandwiches and beer. Will recognized an acquaintance.

"Phineas, how ya doin?" Will hailed his friend.

"Fine, I've got a story to tell you." Phineas was upbeat.

"Great! Meet my friends." Will called out.

"Can I trust your friends with a secret?" Phineas said aside.

"No problem, they are all patriots." Will replied. "Phineas let me introduce you to Rory, Belinda and Helen."

"Nice to meet you Phineas." all in turn

"Phineas works in the Space program. He and his team are building a rocket to take us to the stars." Will disclosed.

"Wow! That's stupendous!" Rory exclaimed.

"Would you like to hear the story that is about to enfold?" Phineas suggested.

"Sure. We would. Is it something Top Secret? We noticed you whispering to Billy." Helen replied.

"No, but it is best to keep it among ourselves for now. Will says I can trust you." Phineas remarked.

"Agreed." All spoke in unison.

"Will, you remember our talk with Brian about the rocket design?" Phineas began.

"Yes indeed that was very interesting." Will replied.

"Our agents discovered a Naga plot to steal the Nishi technology and our plans for the rocket design." Phineas led them on.

"That does not surprise me. I have seen a lot of suspicious activity in my store." Belinda offered.

"We are well aware of that, as you know, Belinda. We set up a ruse to burn the Nagas in their game of intrigue." Phineas continued.

Helen was curious. "So, you know Belinda?"

"No, we have never met in person but she is trusted in the Nishi network. So keep in mind never any loose words to strangers." Phineas warned.

Rory reached out to her. "Helen, do you feel comfortable about being included?"

"Yes. I am all for protecting my friends against the wiles of the Nagas." Helen replied.

"Ok let me go ahead. I was at the Ramada last weekend for a conference and just happened to meet a lady by the name of Paulina who was very friendly. I invited her into my room where she opened my briefcase while I was sleeping. She sneaked out in the morning with the rocket plans and rushed off with Valentin in his car waiting outside the hotel." Phineas told the story very concisely.

"You let her take the plans for the rocket?" Helen was confused about the ruse.

"Yes, I did, and I hope the Nagas will build and test the prototype soon." Phineas replied.

"But why would you hand over secrets to this lady you just met?" Helen inquired.

"If they do succeed in building the rocket to specifications on the plans Paulina stole, they will be in for a big surprise." Phineas spoke like a fox.

"So are they fake plans?" Helen guessed.

"Let's just say Kaboom!" Phineas grinned widely.

Helen laughed with Rory and Belinda who were waiting for her to get it.

"Brian!" a familiar face showed up

"Bill Witherspoon? Look who rose from the dead!" Brian smiled.

"Yup, they found me in a pile of rubble and put me back together in the hospital." Spoon grinned.

Brian looked at Spoon and gave him a hug. "Gee, I'm glad you are ok. You look very fit." Brian was so glad to see his friend again.

"I'm fit and ready for battle." Spoon stretched and struck a pose to get a laugh.

"Spoon, let me introduce you to my friends, Phineas, Rory, Will, Belinda and Helen."

"How do you do?" Spoon courteously replied.

The friends greeted Spoon and invited him to sit with them for lunch.

"You mentioned something about a battle. Is there something brewing nearby?" Rory was worried about spilling his beer.

"Our town was spared once as you all recall from the Tsunami with the help of barricades engineered by the Nishi. In a few days the National Guard has been informed of an impending invasion here in this very town. We suspect they have knowledge of its strategic importance." Spoon was more concerned about the spilling of blood.

"I suppose I expected this invasion to come eventually. Will we be evacuated? Rory was worried about his bookstore being looted.

"We have another plan. For now we would like you to entertain a few of our Nishi guests. Later, we have arranged underground shelters." Spoon was concerned about the sheltering of people who may soon be homeless.

"Wow I would be pleased to have them." Rory replied.

"We cannot meet them here. What do you suggest?" Spoon was hoping Rory would open his home for the Nishi.

"I have a big place. We could meet there." Rory was going along with Spoon's plan.

"Rory, you will have to excuse me I have to rescue someone." Will had just received a call from his squadron.

"Ok, Will, be careful. I hope to see you later." Rory had never been in combat. Recent events were a shock for him.

"Here they are, just arriving." Spoon addressed his friends.

In strode a company of Nishi warriors adorned in silk garments. Rory and his friends gasped at the sight of the wondrous Nishi, human like in form but so graceful in movement.

"Let me introduce you to our allies in the fight against the Naga. The distinguished Celaeno, one of the Seven Sisters accompanied by Triton, Nereus, Maira, Nemesis and Glaucus." Spoon had met these warriors in battles against the Naga.

Helen admired the male Nishi: Triton, Glaucus and Nereus. They all had a bluish green tinge to their skin as if they belonged to the sea. Rory gazed at the female Nishi exquisite in beauty. Celaeno was dark skinned swarthy with an Olympic physique. Nemesis was fair skinned, blue eyes, tall, very slim and athletic. Maira had a bronze complexion, long dark hair and the body of a goddess.

Soon, they all began to mingle and talk.

Nereus explained to his hosts that he expected the battle to be a show of force of K'ny Storm troopers down Main Street after they quelled the local police and the Guard. The Dragon ship would not bomb the University as long as it was not used as a base of operations. But to be on the safe side all noncombatants were urged to enter a bomb shelter underground. The Nishi would accompany the Guard and give them a surprise. There was a beep coming from a radio... Spoon answered the urgent call.

"Hello Sargent Witherspoon speaking."

"Help we are being attacked by Dragons breathing fire into our ranks." Gunfire and artillery rounds could be heard in the background.

"Identify and show your location." Spoon replied.

"Private Ortiz 2nd Battalion North of town sector A." Ortiz sounded shaken up.

"What do you have as weapons?" Spoon replied in a firm clear voice.

"M4's and grenade launchers." Ortiz spoke sporadically for gunfire was heard in the background.

"Use them, shoot the critters down. Hold your position. We will send help pronto." Spoon ordered in a clear voice.

"We are being overrun. There must be fifty Dragons and hundreds of Naga Storm troopers advancing. Out." Ortiz exclaimed as if he was being attacked directly.

"We had better suit up and move out." Spoon addressed all who would fight.

"Sargent Witherspoon, I believe this is a diversionary tactic. A Naga commander has arrived with a retinue of his pets to terrorize the inhabitants. They are no real military threat but they pose a danger to the civilians. It is a tactic to divert our force from the main attack." Nereus spoke calmly.

"What do you propose? I am charged with protecting the populace." Spoon was listening.

Nereus had a plan. "I will stay behind here with Celaeno and Glaucus to await the main attack. We will be needed to coordinate from this location. I ask that Brian stay with us as a local contact."

"Granted. Hope to see you soon." Spoon had confidence in Nereus.

"May the blessing of Amaterasu be upon you." Nereus gave Spoon a Nishi blessing of peace.

"There are suits for you here. Take the helmets. You will need them to protect against the fire breathing Dragons. They can scorch close to 30 meters." Nereus leader of the Nishi

"Don't get fried buddy. Put on the helmet." Brian warned Rory.

"I'm more worried about those nasty velociraptors." Rory was afraid of alien creatures.

"Do you want me to come along? I have no fighting experience." Helen felt out of place.

"Do you want to fight?" Spoon gave her the option.

"Yes, I do." Helen was forthright.

"Then come with us, Belinda will show you how to use a weapon." Spoon recruited her into his troop.

"Don't worry about your fear Helen. I will show you how to fire the Nishi blaster or you could use a machine gun." Belinda was a veteran fighter.

"Thanks, actually I think shooting Nagas will be fun." Helen was a hunter.

"Let's roll!" Spoon got the troop moving.

Eight combatants embarked onto the large transport. Rory, Helen, Belinda and the Nishi, Maira, Triton and Nemesis. Spoon and Maira rode upfront.

Triton gave Rory a photon blaster. "Do you know how to use it?" It was a dangerous weapon.

"Slide this back and push this button on the side. First push this safety lever before firing." Triton carefully trained the novice.

"Got it. What is that you are holding?" Rory's eyes were fixed on a shiny object Triton was holding.

"It's a trishula. Sort of like a lightning bolt." Triton explained the best he could.

"So you hurl it and it hits like a bolt of lightning." Rory imagined something from a science fiction thriller.

"Yes. I see you catch on quick." Triton complemented him.

"So what does this blaster do?" Rory felt powerful holding the blaster.

"It unleashes a beam of laser light like liquid lightning." Triton said with a British accent.

"So, do I hold the trigger or push for short bursts?" Rory was eager to confront the foe.

"Use short bursts on troopers and hold longer for a transport." Triton responded.

Rory wondered about his fate in battle. "What happens if I get hit by a cosmic blaster?"

"Your suit will protect you and recycle the energy to recharge your blaster. Just connect it to your suit with this cable here." Triton showed Rory how to protect himself.

"Wow that's amazing! The enemy will recharge my weapon." Rory was relieved to be wearing such a suit of armor.

Spoon parked the transport on Lee Avenue and the troop marched a block west on Suydam Street toward an old stone church on the corner of Suydam and Livingston streets. A few blocks north he could see K'ny troops approaching along the streets. From this point, Spoon could seek the Guard troops and radio air support as needed.

"Weapons at the ready. Put on your helmets." Spoon commanded. "Hostiles are approaching our position!"

Rory, Helen and Belinda readied their M4's. Spoon carried a missile launcher and a revolver. Maira held a sword by her side. Triton held his trishula, and Nemesis held a whip.

Behind the church, a Dragon emerged glared at the seven. It screamed a deathly roar and poured out its wrath of fire upon them. The seven hid behind a rock wall as the fire burst forth. The Naga Dragon with wings outspread whipped its tail, and drew back its long neck, as his jaws opened wide baring a row of teeth like daggers. A long, forked tongue emerged feeling the air, nostrils wide and deep like caves sniffed out the hiding prey. Naga was hungry for human flesh. It was the prize of victory.

Nemesis felt the intense heat, but suddenly it cooled as the gel inside her suit repelled the heat. She stood and faced the Dragon, looking it into its glaring eyes. Drool dripped from Naga's fangs as she savored the taste to come. Naga took a step closer, stomping the ground before Nemesis, and showing her superior bulk and strength. She brought her wings around to circle Nemesis and arched her neck for the strike of death. Would Nemesis sacrifice herself to save her comrades? Naga looked into Nemesis' icy blue eyes and saw reflection pools, and herself in a whirlpool of ice, a cold blue vortex descending into an abysmal sea.

Nemesis cracked her whip toward the Dragon and ensnared its neck. The whip turned icy blue, and its essence permeated the neck, turning it into ice, that crept into every part of the Dragon. Within seconds the Dragon was a sculpture in ice, frozen in time with its last shriek. K'ny troops who witnessed the sight, retreated in fear away from Nemesis. Triton hurled his trishula into the belly of the beast. In a burst of lightning, it shattered like glass. Helen and Rory were struck with wonder at the feats of Nemesis and Triton. Spoon led the seven forward to meet the Guard. As they marched up the street, they saw the burnt corpses of many soldiers of the Guard. Unfortunately many did not have protective armor against such intense heat. Soldiers of the Guard came out of hiding as Spoon's troop advanced northeast on Livingston Avenue.

Spoon identified soldiers of the Guard. "Soldier! Are you and your squad ok?"

"Yes, Sargent. What remains of our platoon are ok but, many were lost in the firefight, and I mean fire. Sargent Brad Gallagher reporting for duty sir." Brad seemed confused.

"Thanks but I am not your commanding officer. I understand you were attacked by a fire breathing Dragon." Spoon attempted to put Brad back on track.

"Our commander Lieutenant Brown was killed in action, fried actually. None of us have helmets, so they took us by surprise." Brad explained what happened to his troop.

"We just learned of the new Naga tactics this morning, so no helmets were issued to the Guard. Do you have any word of other units?" Spoon inquired.

"There are other artillery units in action with infantry support northeast of this position. As far as I know, they took out at least half the Naga infantry of 20,000 and transports but lost two Howitzers and about 5,000 men. It's been very costly." Brad was exhausted.

"What equipment and personnel do we have in action now?" Spoon needed strategic information.

"Last time I recall about 5,000 personnel, two Paladin Howitzers, a M142 Rocket launcher, and a big M270 Rocket launcher. Apache gunships took out seven transports and one Dragon ship." Brad worked with a radio operator who had knowledge of tactical support positions.

Spoon was relieved to hear the news. "Great to hear we still have a fighting chance against some ten thousand K'ny and another Dragon ship on the way."

"Two Dragon ships landed across the river, and there may be another in hiding nearby." Brad provided more vital information.

"Is that a sniper rifle you're carrying in that case, Sargent?" Spoon was observant.

"Yes. I knocked off nineteen Nagas from a perch before they started to bombard my post." Brad was proud of his kills.

Spoon had a plan to consolidate forces. "Well done Brad. We have to move out. I plan to retreat back to the old stone church and get helmets for your squad."

"That would be a lifesaver." Brad needed a rest.

"Ok troop, let's move out. Back to the old stone church." Spoon ordered his troop.

In step, Brad and his squad of forty followed Spoon and his troop back to the old church where they met the Dragon.

Brad said. "Sargent Witherspoon, I would like to introduce to you Corporal Elakshi Patel. She is our ranking member and logistics technical support. She can fill you in with more information about troop movements."

"Hello Elakshi, I am glad to have you here alive, as well as your company." Spoon shook her hand.

"Thanks Sargent. I will update you on our troops and the foe's position and strength." Elakshi spoke with a Hindi accent.

"Thanks! That will be invaluable to us." Spoon was grateful.

"Have you served previously in the Guard here? Elakshi thought Spoon reminded her of someone.

"This is my third deployment in New Jersey. First, I served in the battle of Newark, and then in the Tsunami evacuation. Then I served in the battle of Portland or rather I survived." Spoon humbly stated.

"Now, I recall hearing about you. You are a legend in the Guard!" Elakshi now remembered hearing stories of a hero.

"Oh come now, that's just because I was rescued and made a speech. I am glad that I can fight another day. You are walking with legends behind the two of us. They have come a long way to fight on our side in the battle for Oceanus. They are the Nephalai of the Nishi." Spoon wanted to shine the light on his allies.

"Nephalai? What do you mean? Are they warriors of the Nishi with special powers?" Elakshi thought they might be superhuman.

"You could say that. Wait till you see them in action. They are unbelievable." Spoon replied.

Spoon received a call from base about a Naga outpost across the Raritan in Johnson Park. Air support was on its way to intercept an incoming Dragon ship coming from the Northeast over the Atlantic.

"Belinda, can you escort Elakshi and her squad to the transport and get helmets for all of them? There should be plenty and get surplus ammo as well." Spoon told her urgently.

"Whiskey Papa, we need air support now. There must be a Dragon ship nearby that transported these troops and menacing Dragons. Over." Spoon used code to reach a pilot.

"Roger Whiskey Bravo. It must be hiding somewhere. We cannot find it on radar. Over." Will Powers replied.

"10-4, I will contact you of troop movements and any alien UFO's if sighted. Out." Spoon replied.

"Roger." Will confirmed.

Rory shouted as he saw a Dragon ship hover over a building just northeast of the Temple. Spoon readied his grenade launcher.

"Whiskey Bravo, bogey spotted over St. Mary's on Remsen 40.48N 74,45W. Over." Spoon called on his radio.

"Wilco Papa Whiskey." Will answered.

K'ny troops appeared out of a side street and fired on the squad. Rory was stunned by a cosmic ray blaster. Helen fired her photon gun at the K'ny. One fell as the others ran for cover. Sword in hand, Maira ran after the K'ny.

"Maira, you are breaking ranks!" Spoon was furious.

"Don't worry about her. She is a trained fighter." Triton calmed him down

"But we may need her here. We are few." Spoon complained about the lack of discipline.

"Soon there will be fewer K'ny." Nemesis grinned.

In a matter of seconds, Maira tracked down the K'ny and engaged the foe. Spoon led his troop to support Maira. K'ny were firing at Maira but she dodged the blasts and fended them off with her sword. With lightning speed, she attacked the foe, cutting the first in the thigh, and then another in the neck. She moved like a cheetah, slicing the enemy down before they could react. Soon the entire troop of twenty were wounded and out of action. She raised her sword up high as it turned blue and light emanated from her.

A Dragon with a rider dived from on high and swept down upon Maira. Helen readied her photon gun and shot the Dragon in the belly. Nemesis smiled and put her arm around Helen.

"Well done." Nemesis complemented her. "You may be an Oceanid yet."

"Yes, she does have promise." Triton concurred.

"Where did you learn to shoot like that?" Spoon was surprised.

"I don't know. I just reacted from instinct." Helen downplayed her part.

"Rory, carry on with your assignment. These soldiers need helmets!" Spoon yelled.

With the squad fully protected, Spoon employed the soldiers inside the old church. Brad found a perch to look for advancing K'ny troops. Elakshi accompanied Brad to get a better position to spy on troop positions and GPS tracking. There was silence for a time and the squad settled down for rest and food.

Closer to the river, Naga commander Budi was frustrated by a stall in the advance of his troops. He was a tall Naga male of the Biru clan and he sported an orange crest. An educated person, he had studied the Buku Takdir and was critical of this invasion campaign. He was convinced after three head-to-head battles with the humans that the K'ny and Naga tactics were no match for their adversaries. He had barely escaped capture after the loss of his Dragon ship in Portland.

Apparently, sabotage and terror tactics to create chaos and threaten the population were the only way to defeat the humans, so he thought. In this campaign Budi introduced Dragons to terrorize the civilians, use them as hostages and hide among them. The opening of the campaign worked out well. Many humans who could be sold as slaves were captured. But to his amazement many of the civilians were armed and shot down his troops who had failed to put on armor. Budi unleashed Dragons upon the neighborhoods to flush them out and burn them alive. The humans retaliated fiercely shooting down three Dragons and their riders with rifles. Many of the humans fled out of town to escape the Dragons and K'ny troops. Next a salvo of rockets and artillery shells were fired at the Dragon ship, which was destroyed on the ground by the missile attack. The transports were wasted. Helicopter gunships rained fire down on his position, cutting down advancing K'ny troops. Infantry soldiers pinned down his advance with rapid machine gun fire. From his position in downtown Brunswick, Budi ordered his troops to fight house to house and follow up the advance of the Nyala, the cavalry who sent incendiaries into the foe.

Thud, thud, and then thud again. Spoon heard the shots ring out from up in the belfry. Brad was taking out K'ny mercenaries one by one. The old church took hits from incendiary missiles, but they missed the belfry tower.

"Rory get Brad and Elakshi down from there before they get hit!" Spoon yelled.

Spoon got the squad together for a conference. Together they decided to spearhead an attack on the incendiary batteries. Corporal Elakshi Patel contacted other battalions for a coordinated assault. Batteries would no longer launch if the Nyala were extinguished. Units across town closed in on an open green space behind the Brunswick Public Library.

"Corporal Patel, have you contacted all units for coordinated fire?" Spoon was implementing a coordinated assault from Central Command.

"Yes, they are ready to fire on command. Lieutenant Ron Henderson of the 50th Brigade gives you the command to order fire when ready. He has rocket launcher, and says to stand clear south of position. He needs coordinates of enemy position." Elakshi alerted Spoon.

"Belinda! Have you honed coordinates of the batteries?" Spoon inquired urgently.

"Yes, we have a fix on them." Belinda reported in an instant.

"Ok send to Elakshi." Spoon replied.

"Elakshi, send coordinates to all units." Spoon gave the command.

Belinda could see Naga batteries and K'ny troops loading projectiles from her position on top of Lord Stirling School.

"Be prepared to move in and fire on K'ny when the smoke clears." Spoon ordered.

"Break...Batteries taken out. Elakshi alerted Ron. Do you copy Romeo Hotel?"

"Roger, Echo Papa, move in for kill. Uglies (Apache Helos) assist." Lieutenant Henderson ordered coordinated assault.

"Spoon Romeo Hotel 10-4." Elakshi confirmed assault ready to Spoon.

"Move out. Fire on my signal. Signal is Kilo Kill Kilo."
Spoon said to his squad.

Some one hundred or more K'ny assembled in the
green took fire from units stationed north along Morris
Avenue. Units swung west around Livingston Avenue
and east around George Street leaving only south as a
way out. K'ny troops ran for cover in between houses
on Welton Street and raced down Lee Street.

"All units cease fire." Lieutenant Henderson called to
all units via radio except Spoon's position.

Silence pervaded the smoke-filled air.

"Kilo Kill Kilo!" Spoon ordered his squad.

Spoon's platoon opened fire on the K'ny who were
running scared. Many poured into a large complex on
Livingston Street identified as a Naga outpost since the
invasion days ago.

"Command Romeo Hotel requesting airstrike on
hardened target south of your position." Spoon called
Ron, his commanding officer.

"Roger that. Call in coordinates to Cobra Delta Niner
one click." Lieutenant Henderson approved his
request.

"Cobra Delta Niner requesting Airstrike on hardened
target N 40.49 W 74.447 Over." Spoon called pilot of
Apache gunship.

"Roger that. Cleared Hot. One click to kill zone."
Captain Daredevil Dick replied with glee.

Belinda caught a Cobra Gunship above treetop level
coming fast from the southwest. A Dragon ship rose
above treetop at northeast sector a long way off moving
fast to intercept Cobra gunship. It fired thermite
missiles at the Cobra, but the Cobra dispersed flak,
spun away, and fired sidewinders at Dragon ship,

scoring hits on its port side. An A-10 warthog dove from above on Dragon ship, and fired a burst of 50 caliber into starboard side. The Dragon ship fired cosmic blasters on the A-10. Pilot Lieutenant Powers spun off, blast deflected off his armor. Powers swung around, and fired sidewinders into belly of the Dragon ship. Its underside exploded, splitting in half, and aliens fell to earth. Daredevil Dick in the Cobra swooped down, and fired ordinance on target.

Naga Commander Budi watched his Dragon ship go down in flames. The battle was lost. His troops were retreating back across the river and the enemy was closing in on his position. He was in shock unable to believe defeat was at hand. In desperation he grabbed his attaché Bambang and directed him to drive him to their secret hideout in Belle Mead.

"Bambang, get the Porsche and drive me to my lair." Budi said in desperation.

"Yes sire." Bambang spoke in an Indonesian tongue he had learned from the Riskani.

Bambang brought the Porsche around from a disguised cover. Budi jumped in and made his escape across the River on Route 27. Police identified the speeding vehicle as stolen and gave pursuit. Budi was apprehended at the bridge across the Millstone River. which had a roadblock waiting for him.

Commander Budi, sitting on the back of a patrol car pondered the news he heard about his rivals in the Middle East and other regions of Oceanus. Throughout the Middle East, including Syria, Iraq, Iran, Jordan, Lebanon and Egypt, the Naga forces were strong and stable. There was little opposition to their presence in the region with the exception of Israel. These people fiercely opposed any Naga intrusion into their territory and were protected by the Nishi starship, Gabriel. The Naga forces also extended through North Africa from

Egypt to Morocco. In these regions, the Naga were primarily involved in recruiting young men and women to join the Naga cause.

In the south of Africa, Nagas were searching for diamonds which they needed for space technology. Naga traders bargained diamond merchants in the black market or took over diamond mines completely. The pirating of diamonds in Australia was closed to them due to the defeat of the Naga in the Pacific theater of war. Japan had a strong Nishi presence with a starship on call to defend the Western Pacific. Much of the Asian continent was in the dominion of the Nagas.

After the Kamchatka invasion, Russia, China and North Korea joined forces with the Nagas. They saw the Naga invasion as an opportunity to overthrow the western powers. By gaining the Nagas as an ally they perceived they could take over the western Pacific region and the rest of Asia. This coalition of Naga allies in the western Pacific threatened Australia. The Nagas wanted the diamond mines of Australia. Naga forces were making incursions into Europe and a confrontation was expecting soon. Budi had not heard any news of Naga activity in South America other than a presence in Columbia. The main focus of the Naga strategy was an attack on the USA. The East coast was devastated by the tsunami leaving the entire coast swept of civilization but the Americans fought even more fiercely. The capital was relocated to Denver and the Western States stood firm against the threat of Nagas invading from Mexico. It was in the Midwest where the Nagas had a stronghold in cities suffering from economic depression.

Budi wondered why the humans fought against the Nagas when they offered them a new vision of dominion in the galaxy. He had studied the sacred texts of Buki Takdir and remembered his own human ancestor who had married the Naga queen and sired a new dynasty, a new species. These humans were very clever and resourceful and they had allies with the Nishi. The Nishi had ruined his plans of victory before the invasion of Oceanus began.

Budi watched the Naga flagship surrender to the Nishi. Defeat at the hands of the Nishi was humiliating. Fully one third of the Naga fleet was destroyed or captured in the battle of the Stratosphere above Oceanus. Budi abandoned ship aboard a Dragon ship as did two thirds of the fleet to continue the invasion. All starships left the solar system of Helios for the refuge of the home planet. Where was the leadership? Why did Admiral Tolpiltzin abandon ship without orders to fight on? Budi fumed with disappointment and anger. But then he had a brilliant idea, why not play into their weaknesses? Terror tactics had not worked very well. Corruption among public officials was as rampant as ever. He would arrange to have human politicians seduced by Nagas in their sex escorting service.

At the scene of the battle near the Brunswick library, Spoon's troop watched the building sheltering the K'ny troops disintegrate into rubble. There was silence after the dust cleared and no K'ny was in sight.

"Spoon, I didn't know Will was a fighter pilot." Helen remarked.

"He kept the secret from us. He is a modest guy." Spoon replied.

"Will didn't want Tatiana to know that he was a weekend warrior." Belinda figured Tatiana was a gossiper.

"Brad, where did you learn to shoot like that?" Spoon was glad to have a trained sniper on his squad.

"I was trained at Army Sniper School Fort Benning, Georgia." Brad replied.

"Wow that must be some experience. Were you deployed after training?" Spoon thought he might want to train as a sniper.

"I did a tour in Afghan, survived. That was enough for me." Brad felt he needed a rest from all the bloodshed.

"It must of have been rough in Afghan. What did you do when you came home?" Spoon admired Brad's service record.

"I couldn't find any good work when I came home, and I had trouble adjusting to civilian life. After a while, I got a job trucking goods 'cross country from Pittsburg to a place outside of LA." Brad had felt abandoned when he came home.

"So how did you end up here in Jersey?" Spoon wondered about Brad's wanderings.

"Long story really, got into trouble with these Naga folks. My boss Larry, who owned the trucking company, had a deal with them. He was my buddy in high school. We went to heavy metal concerts together with our girlfriends. We distrusted the Nishi and their peaceful ways. He told me the Nagas were liberators who would make us rich. He was supplying food to the Nagas from recruits who rampaged through local markets and farms through the Midwest. For all the driving I did 'cross country, I got chump change for food and fuel. Storekeepers, farmers and bystanders were shot outright for resisting. People were dragged out into the street and hacked to pieces.

"There was no trading with the Nagas. They sought utter dominion and strode about taking whatever they pleased. They dealt food, hardware, electronics and women for sex slaves. In their territory I kept my mouth shut and watched Larry speak to the Nagas called K'ny in a strange tongue. I came to despise Larry for deceiving me and longed for a way out. At night memories of my childhood came to me of my mom and dad reading me the Bible and taking me to Sunday school." Brad was honest and upfront about his past life.

"So how did you escape from this hell?" Helen sympathized with his plight.

"I met a traveler one day who asked me to join him. We disappeared into the forest and hiked on the Appalachian Trail. He played music at night, old folk songs by the campfire. Hikers came to visit us to hear the music. Harmony of the wilderness brought me peace and understanding." Brad told of his enlightenment.

"Did you ever go back home to see your family?" Belinda wondered why he travelled so much.

"I can hardly bear to tell you but our neighborhood in Pittsburgh was destroyed." Brad held back the tears.

"Sorry to hear that." Belinda comforted him.

"So I joined the National Guard to defend our people and here I am today." Brad wanted to put the past behind him.

"We are sure glad you did buddy." Rory supported him.

"I miss my buddies who were killed in battle. So many deaths, so much destruction at the hands of the Nagas, I wonder if it will ever end." Brad said.

"Yes the death toll today was high, over 5,000 casualties and perhaps as much as 1000 mortally wounded." Elakshi reported the reality of the battle to the squad.

"You can visit your friends at CASH (Combat Military Support Hospital). It is safe now." Spoon disclosed to Brad.

A Dragon ship appeared above treetop level and began bombarding downtown with incendiaries east of Spoon's position. It shifted its orientation and moved toward the library.

"Hey, it's heading toward us! Take cover!" Spoon shouted.

A Nishi Cruiser, far bigger than the Dragon ship, emerged from the clouds and targeted the Dragon ship with a beam of intense purple light. The Dragon ship stopped in its tracks and careened into a wooded area across the river. The Nishi Cruiser followed its course and landed nearby.

"Saddle up troops. We are taking a hike toward that Cruiser." Spoon ordered.

"Wow! That was close!" Rory was scared thinking he was a character in the War of the Worlds.

"Who are these guys in the UFO?" Brad was amazed to see such an immense craft.

"That is a Nishi Class I Cruiser. Here is your chance to meet Nishis in person." Rory recovered from his daydreaming.

"Brad, you have been fighting alongside Nishis in our company." Belinda informed him.

"Really, I haven't noticed anyone unusual except a few in this squad?" Brad replied with consternation.

"Meet Maira, Triton and Nemesis, Nephalai of the Nishi." Rory replied congenially.

"It's a pleasure to meet you folks. I never heard of Nephalai before." Brad greeted the strangers graciously.

"It's our pleasure to meet you Brad. You are a brave soldier. We commend you to the Nishi. Nephalai are transcendent Nishi, who have risen above existence. We are here to protect your world." Maira spoke in a lilting voice.

Brad had never met such a beautiful dazzling woman before.

"I would like to know more about you and your world." Brad replied with fervor.

"You are welcome to take a trip on our starship if you like." Triton welcomed him.

Brad marveled at the sight of Triton. He looked like a superhero from comic books with a large head full of curls, aquamarine eyes and a blueish tinge to his somewhat scaly skin. He was carrying a forked weapon that looked like a spear to catch fish.

"Triton, do you catch fish with that forked spear?" Brad asked naively.

Triton and the others laughed.

"It's called a trishula. It has the power of a thunderbolt." Triton spoke grandly in a booming voice.

Smiling Nemesis stood alongside Triton. Her violet eyes and milky white skin was very alluring. Brad looked on in admiration.

"Hello. Brad, I am glad to meet you. Let me take you to the starship." Nemesis came alongside him.

Brad took her hand willingly. He felt her soft tender skin and walked like he was floating on air. He wanted to know what she meant by transcendence but for now he was eager to find out about this spaceship and the Nishi.

Spoon's troop hiked down Easton Avenue until they came to a baseball park. The Cruiser had its landing struts set over the field, and a ladder of sorts was emerging from the bottom of the saucer-like spacecraft. It was immense, about 760 feet in diameter and ninety feet high. As they approached, the thrusters were entering the body and disappearing from view.

A door opened on the bottom of the Cruiser and a company of soldiers emerged. In their midst behind the first company a young lady with long black hair led a Dragon with a bridle.

"Leucothea!" Maira shouted cheerfully.

"Maira! Helios shines on you!" Leucothea yelled as she led the Dragon out of the ship.

Spoon recognized the young lady. "Judy!"

"Spoon! I have come to see you my love." Leucothoe cried out to him.

Spoon wasn't sure about running to see her with a Dragon in tow.

"It's safe Spoon. The Dragon is tame." Leucothoe assured him.

"So you are taming Dragons now?" Spoon chided her.

"Oh, Spoon. They are a lot like horses. You just have to know how to handle them." Leucothoe winked.

Spoon strode up to Leucothoe. She put her hand on the neck of the Dragon and whispered. The Dragon relaxed and sat for her master. Leucothoe put her arms around Spoon and kissed him. Maira came up to greet the couple.

"So, Leucothoe, you go by the name of Judy?" Maira inquired.

"It is my adopted name here on Oceanus." Leucothoe attested.

"Hello, Leucothoe. Where were you when all the fighting broke out?" Nemesis bantered with the upstart.

"I was on the other side of town fighting Dragons. They are not all so easily tamed like this one." Leucothoe replied.

"How did you manage to tame this creature?" Triton taunted the Dragon rider.

"It wasn't easy. At the start of the battle, a Dragon ship disembarked thirteen Dragons with riders. The Guard troops were not equipped to defend themselves against the fiery blasts, but they did manage to bring a few down. In the fray of battle, I killed a Dragon with my sword. From then on the other Dragons stayed clear of me. This one lost its rider, and I jumped on its back. Instead of killing it, I decided to whisper charms and stroked its neck. Soon, it obeyed my commands, and I bought it into safe custody." Leucothoe told with braggadocio.

Lieutenant Jameson stepped forward to greet Sgt. Witherspoon as Spoon saluted his commanding officer. Lieutenant Henderson returned his salute.

"Sargent Witherspoon, I commend you on your leadership in this action. Captain Armstrong has conferred upon you the rank of Staff Sergeant, troop citations and silver stars for all in your platoon." Lieutenant Jameson said in a commanding voice.

Lieutenant Jameson pinned the Silver Star on Spoon's chest and presented him with the staff Sargent insignia.

"Spoon, we are all very proud of the gallantry of you and your troop. You have save many lives and together we have defeated the foe. Captain Armstrong will be here shortly to greet your platoon." Lieutenant Jameson spoke as a friend.

"Thank you, sir." Spoon replied respectfully.

"Spoon, I am so proud of you." Leucothoe came alongside her man.

"Frankly, dear, I am amazed at your accomplishments." Spoon put his arm around her.

"Sir, have you heard any word of the Navy pilot Will Powers?" Helen spoke to Lieutenant Jameson.

"I understand that he has returned to Naval Operations Earle and is on duty call for an upcoming battle in Philadelphia." Lieutenant Jameson responded.

"I'm glad he survived this horrific battle." Helen spoke with relief.

"Yes, dear. He is doing fine but you may not be hearing from him soon."

Lieutenant Jameson spoke kindly.

"Thank you so much, sir." Helen replied respectfully.

"Spoon, get some rest for you and your troop. I have to lead these men into search and rescue teams." Lieutenant Jameson gave Spoon and his squad liberty.

"Aye Aye, Sir" Spoon saluted his senior officer.

Lieutenant Jameson led the company ahead and divided them into squads to search for wounded soldiers and any K'ny troops in hiding. Four more companies led by sergeants followed after him.

"Hey, dude, what are you waiting for? Come on aboard." Koko waved at his friend Rory.

Commander Ulani emerged to greet the troops.

"Welcome aboard all you brave fighters. I am concerned that the fighting is not over. We have just found another Dragon ship on our screens heading this way. We ask you all to enter the Cruiser for your safety. We believe this enemy ship will unleash its fleet of Terrosoars, delta wing fighters." Ulani spoke in a resounding voice.

Friendly troops under the Guard from all combat units in the town entered the Cruiser before the confrontation from the air.

"Prepare for liftoff. Secure yourselves in your seats." Nishi officer stated.

The thrusters emerged from the Cruiser and began firing as the landing gear was retracted into the ship. Quickly, the Cruiser spun off in the direction of the Dragon ship detected. On the screen inside the Operations Bridge, small red triangles could be seen in formation heading toward the town. The Dragon ship was behind and heading in the opposite direction away from the town. Three groups of blue triangles were converging on the red triangles.

"Captain Armstrong, these red triangles are the Terrosoar fighters released from the Dragon ship." Ulani pointed at the Naga fleet.

"There must be hundreds of fighters in that fleet." stated Captain Armstrong

"Commander Ulani, are the blue triangles our jets in pursuit of the red triangles, the Naga Fleet?" Spoon asked.

"That is correct, Sargent. Your fighters should be able to handle the enemy." stated Ulani

On the screen, missiles could be seen firing from the blue jets toward the red jets. Already the blue had found the enemy and were knocking them out of the sky. Evidently the red could not detect the blue from a distance. Then some of the red ones turned away to the right and left as the center stayed on course. Spoon noticed the red jets flying in twists and turns with much agility. A few of the blue jets were hit with missiles from the red foes and went down. Other blue jets followed the red ones and shot them down. The center force of the red ones continued to rush toward their target right in the path of the Cruiser.

"Fire all photonic blasters on the incoming red targets!" ordered Commander Ulani

On the screen, Spoon looked at a burst of light like lightning strike the incoming red jets. As the photon blast hit the incoming jets, they faltered and fell in a swirling spiral toward the ground and exploded on impact. A shout from the troops hailed the victory.

"Hurray! Ooh rah!" Many cheers erupted from the audience aboard.

"The battle is not over yet. We have to catch up to that Dragon ship. Set coarse to intercept, Lieutenant!" ordered Commander Ulani

On the big screen, Spoon could see the Dragon ship taking in a few of the red jets escaping from the battle followed by the blue jets in pursuit. A flash of purple rays shot from the Dragon ship toward the blue jets. The blue jets were stunned but the radiation was deflected by the fullerene armor. Nonetheless it slowed the blue jets down. The Cruiser was closing in on the Dragon ship which was now over the Atlantic Ocean heading northeast. An array of purple rays shot from the Dragon ship toward the Cruiser. Spoon was worried, this time the deadly purple rays would blast the ship in a moment. The cosmic ray blast hit the Cruiser and was glowing around the outside of the ship then it was gone in an instant.

"Not to worry troops. Those cosmic rays just gave us a boost of energy. Carbon nanotubes in the ship's hull will recycle that energy and shoot it right back at them." stated Commander Ulani

"Lieutenant, set our blaster on stun. We want to capture the ship and take the crew prisoner." stated Commander Ulani

"Aye, Aye, Sir." Lt. Jameson responded.

Spoon watched the big screen. The Dragon ship zigzagged in its course to evade capture. Another shot of purple rays hit the Cruiser but to no effect. Then a white blast hit the Dragon ship. It faltered and fell toward the sea below but it managed to make a safe splash down.

"Open a channel to the Dragon ship, Lieutenant." ordered Commander Ulani

"Aye, Aye, Sir." replied Lt. Jameson at the Communications controls center.

Commander Ulani pushed a button and activated another small screen for viewing incoming communication.

"Naga Commanding officer, this is Commander Ulani of the Nishi Cruiser Orion. Do you read me?"

"Aye, this is Commander Bangga of His Majesties Dragon Vessel VII. Congratulations on your victory, Nishi warrior."

"Victory is not in my hands, Commander Bangga. I am here to demand the surrender of you, your ship and all your crew. Do you accept these terms?" Commander Ulani

"Under what conditions, Nishi warrior? I will go down with my ship fighting to the last man!" cried Commander Bangga disdainfully.

"Then you and your crew will drown in the sea and be eaten by the fish." Ulani stated.

Bangga cringed at the thought of being eaten by fish and possibly some monster. He wallowed in self-pity and raged at his crew.

"You have one minute to answer to my demand. Unconditional Surrender!" demanded Commander Ulani. He waited as seconds ticked away.

"Very well, I accept your terms." Commander Bangga surrendered.

"You have fifteen minutes to assemble all officers and yourself to leave ship and be put into custody." Commander Ulani instructed. "If you are not ready in time, I will blast a hole in your ship!"

In just under fourteen minutes Commander Bangga emerged from his vessel and waited on a platform outside his ship with his officers. Nishi commandoes in fast attack vessels surrounded the ship and took Commander Bangga and his officers into custody. The Nishi Cruiser landed in the sea nearby and Nishi seaman attached a cable to the Naga ship. Nishi commandoes entered the Dragon ship, placed the crew under guard and took control of the ship.

"Lieutenant, set a heading toward the port of Newark." Commander Ulani ordered in an easy tone.

"Aye, Aye, Sir." replied Lieutenant Jameson

Spoon was amazed at the efficiency and mastery of the Nishi crew. It was clear the Naga were no match for the Nishi, yet the Nishi let the people of Oceanus fight for their planet.

"Sir we have arrived at the Port of Newark." Lieutenant Jameson stated.

"Very well, prepare for landing." Commander Ulani ordered.

"Sir, we have incoming jet fighters on screen. The flight duty officer has identified them as friendly." Ensign reported from radar console.

"Open a channel and prepare hangar for landing." Commander Ulani ordered.

"F-35 is coming in for a landing deck 2." Ensign reported.

On the big screen on the bridge, Rory could see a jet approaching the hangar bay on the side of the ship above the lower deck. It was a full visual display with the flight deck crew ready to guide the aircraft to a landing site. A pilot emerged from the cockpit and took off his helmet. Rory couldn't believe his eyes, it was Lieutenant Will Powers. He must have been in the thick of the fight. Will strode over to the flight crew, shook hands and thanked the crew for their support.

"Say Joe, were you guys watching the fight? How did it go? I think we lost a few fighters. I saw one go down." Swaggering, Will felt his legs getting used to ground.

"We saw it all right, it was a blast. You guys smoked those Terrosoars. The battle is over and we got their Dragon ship." Joe spoke to Will like he was the quarterback of the winning team.

"Wow, I don't see the whole picture just what is buzzing around my jet." Will was glad to hear the news from the guys who kept his plane in the air.

Ray, air deck crewman joined in. "Commander Ulani downed the Dragon ship and captured the Naga commander and his crew."

"Up in the sky I saw the destruction of downtown Brunswick. Many thousands of people must have died in the bombardment. I am worried about friends of mine. They were in the Guard fighting in the street." Will gave them a bird's eye view of the action.

"We picked up the soldiers of the Guard before the air battle. I can escort you to the deck below where they are resting now." A female private offered her assistance.

Will felt the sweat dripping down his face, energy pulsed through his body and thoughts of Tatiana stirred in his mind as he remembered the rubble that was her house on George Street. No conquest in battle would bring her back. He strode forward to meet his friends hoping to see them all alive, but he thought she would not be among them. He reached the duty officer on the deck of the bridge.

"Lieutenant Powers, reporting for duty, sir." Will saluted his fellow officer

"You have earned liberty Will, for a job well done." Lieutenant Jameson replied.

"Thanks. Have you got a report of our pilots downed?" Will asked.

"Yes. Two were rescued from their chutes but unfortunately we lost Lieutenant Wainwright. He was found dead at the scene of the crashed aircraft." Ron replied grimly.

"Too bad," Will said softly. "He was a good man and father of two. He is going to be missed in our company."

"Yes, he was a funny guy and I will miss the poker winnings too." Ron replied.

"Well you could send his wife some if you haven't spent it all." Will responded.

"Be sure of it I will give her seven times that and ask for a charity to help her now that he is gone." Ron attempted a comeback.

"Ron, did you see Sargent Witherspoon and his platoon?" Will inquired.

"Yes, come with me. They are down the hall with the troops." Ron replied.

Will heard gentle music and the sound of water falling as he entered into a large room. Tropical trees reached to a high ceiling diffuse with light. People were resting beside fountains, sitting on benches. He saw a group coming toward him from a path through the dense vegetation.

"Well what do you know, if it ain't Will Powers flyboy!" Rory yelped.

"Hey, slacker. What ya been doing all this time when I've been gettin shot up dude?" Will jived.

"Dude, I was on the ground taken a beatin' and slammin' dem Nagas. It was damn horrific down here with those fire breathin' Dragons and K'ny shootin ray guns at us." Rory complained.

"Hey Will, good to see you all in one piece." Spoon said.

"It's good to see you too brother. Did your entire troop make it through?" Will asked.

"We did just barely with the help of the Nephali, Triton, Nemesis and this lady of mine, Leucothoe." Spoon said.

"Leucothoe? No this is Judy the heroine we have all heard about. She is a fury on the battlefield." Will corrected his friend.

Spoon smiled. "That ain't the only place she is a fury on. She is of the Nephalai and they know her as Leucothoe."

"Well ain't that something. You got a superwoman for a girlfriend. Good luck with that my friend." Will said .

Behind the crowd of onlookers, Will heard a cry. "Will!"

A lady with blond hair came dashing through the crowd.

"Will, oh my darling!"

She rushed to him and put her arms around him. Will embraced her and kissed her tenderly. "I'm so glad to see you honey." whispered Will.

He realized now that it was Helen who loved him. Belinda tugged at Rory and he kissed her. Judy kissed her man Spoon. On the steps facing the garden a guitarist played *Concierto de Aranjuez* to the sounds of birds flying throughout the arboretum. Here was a place of peace and retreat from the onslaught of Nagas fomenting chaos upon Oceanus.

XIBALBAN THREAT

Commander Ulani had a plan in hand to deal a blow to the Naga base located on the dark side of the moon. This base was heavily fortified with underground installations from which Dragon ships were launched. It was discovered that Naga starships were operating between the Moon base and one on Mars.

Commander Ulani received a transmission from a Nishi Cruiser in proximity of the Naga Moon base on a reconnaissance mission.

"Tangaroa! Tangaroa! Come in!" Ulani called.

"This is the Nishi Starship Tangaroa."

"Commander Ulani, we request your support in lieu of imminent attack from numerous unknown vessels." Captain Nobuo uttered urgently.

"What is your condition? Have you sustained any damage?" Ulani inquired.

"There is a breach in our outer hull. We have been hit by multiple blasts from at least a dozen unknown vessels." Nobuo reported.

"I will direct our vessel to assist at full speed to intercept the foe. I order you to retreat and head to port for repairs. Do not engage the enemy further." Ulani ordered.

"Aye, Aye Commander." Nobuo replied.

Ulani arrived at the scene of the battle but the screen showed nothing but floating wreckage.

"Lieutenant Yori, zoom in on that large piece center with logo." Ulani ordered.

The enlarged image clearly showed the Nishi insignia.

Ulani and his comrades were downcast. It was evident that the entire crew may have been lost.

"Lieutenant Yori, raise a signal for Captain Nobuo and crew. A few may have escaped in pods."

Yori sent transmission. "Captain Nobuo, do you hear us?"

"We can hear you loud and clear Nishi meat. Are you ready to fight or are you going to turn tail and run?" Komodo taunted.

The transmission was heard by Commander Ulani though it sounded like a digital monotone rendering of the Xibalban reptilian tongue. Ulani did not respond but silently gave orders to his crew to engage.

"Lieutenant Chieko, turn on vessel cloak and arm for assault on pirates. Alert Battle stations for attack." Ulani ordered.

"Aye, Aye Commander." Chieko replied.

"Lieutenant Yori, enable Ultra to detect cloaked pirate vessels and blast when found." Ulani ordered.

"Aye, Aye Commander." Yori replied.

The big screen on the bridge illuminated thirteen pirate vessels closing in on the *Tangaroa*. Ulani was not deterred and held his ground.

"Fire at all 13 at once!" ordered Ulani.

The screen showed bright purple rays targeting the thirteen vessels. Three in the front of the formation slowed to a halt with breaches in their hulls. The ten following behind in a chevron formation were shaken but not breached. The four in the rear veered off, disappeared from the screen and made their escape. The three behind the damaged vessels in front surged forth and attacked the Nishi starship with blasts.

Ulani and his crew felt the ship shake and rumble from the blast.

"Report damage reports, Lieutenant Yoshio." Ulani ordered.

"No damage sustained Commander. Our glorious ship *Taniwha* is ready Sir." Yoshio replied.

"Fire on the remaining six vessels!" Ulani ordered.

The screen on the bridge showed bright purple rays targeting all six vessels. The three in front were hit directly, their hulls were breached. They were dead in space. The other three behind were also hit but veered off and disappeared from screen.

"Prepare to board. We will take only leaders prisoner. Put the rest to the sword. Fire another volley into the damaged vessels." Ulani ordered.

The screen showed blue rays targeting six damaged pirate vessels. Repeated volleys destroyed circuitry and weapon systems. Scanning with infrared, showed life signs but many dead were also detected aboard.

"We will show these Xibalbans the folly of attacking a Nishi Starship! Ulani exclaimed.

Nishi warriors launched jets and attached to the pirate vessels. Protected by armor, they blasted into the vessels and attacked the foe with fury. With samurai swords equipped with photonic lasers they lopped off the heads of the Xibalbans.

An ugly reptilian stood with a jagged axe confronting the Nishi warriors. In a garbled translation the reptile with a huge knobby head challenged the lead Nishi warrior Tetsip to a duel.

"Nishi scum I challenge your lead man. Then I will eat him for breakfast." Xiblaban roared.

Tetsip stepped forward without a word, sword at his side.

Growling with his mouth full of teeth, the Xibalban lunged at him from ten meters. Tetsip lifted his sword to meet the reptile's axe. He strained under the heavy blow but twisted around and cut the reptile behind his leg. The reptile groaned and struck again with his axe but missed. Tetsip lopped of his head and kicked it to the side. The Nishi warriors slaughtered the rest of the reptilian pirates and strung up the leaders like chickens. After interrogation they had nothing much to offer the Nishi for information. They were executed, their heads lopped off. A complete scan was made of the pirate vessels to ascertain all its technology. The Nishi warriors returned to the Starship *Taniwha* without a loss of men and only blood on their swords.

"I thank all the crew for your loyalty and bravery in the face of great danger. We cannot bring back our comrades. So now we pray that they may rest and return in the life to come." Ulani commended his crew.

All decks were silent as everyone remembered the fallen warriors.

"Fire on the remaining six pirate vessels. Blow them to dust!" Ulani ordered.

Screen showed no rays but suddenly all six vessels were blown apart and disintegrated.

Commander Ulani alerted Central command of the loss of the Nishi Cruiser *Tiburon* and crew under Captain Nobuo. The loss of the Nishi Cruiser was unprecedented and tragic. The Nishi had not confronted and fought the Xibalbans for centuries. Five hundred years ago Oceanus time, the Xibalbans invaded the Nishi homeland and were repelled but with heavy losses.

Central Nishi Command gave orders to all Cruiser commanders to return to Oceanus atmosphere where Xibalban pirate ships could not cloak. They were also ordered not to engage more than one Xibalban vessel at a time. All helioports were alerted to the Xibalban threat. Nishi starships were gathering to defeat the Xibalban menace. Nothing but an X1 pulsar could penetrate the armor of a Nishi starship. The battle of the Naga Moon base would continue with Nishi starships.

Spoon and Judy were saddened by the destruction of the *Tangaroa*. There dear friends Eric, Zoe, Tammy and Mike were aboard before the attack. They had seen them depart from Portland before the battle with Nagas began. Al this time Judy and Spoon had thought they were safe and on their way to Tlalocan to rescue Maia. Maia was a friend of Eric. She was kidnapped along with members of her congregation after her church was flooded by the Northeast Tsunami.

Meanwhile aboard the Nishi starship *Calypso,* Admiral Mitsuo announced to crew and passengers: "We are arriving at Nishi helioport, Oceanus V, just outside the heliosphere."

Upon arrival at the helioport, First mate Galatea, a young Nishi woman, stepped aboard the Calypso. "Hello Admiral Mitsuo and crew. It is good to see you. To you brave crew members and those newcomers to space exploration, I will be your teacher for the duration of our journey.

Galatea explained to crew: "We are now 120 astronomical units from Helios, your sun, and outside the magnetic field of it. At one tenth the speed of light within the solar system, the Starship has reached the helioport in seventeen days. There has been no sign of the Naga ship we have been pursuing. Evidently it has slipped past our sentries."

Galatea read a passage from the Enuma Elish:

"When the skies above were not yet named

Nor earth below pronounced by name,

Apsu, the first one, their begetter,

And maker Tiamat, who bore them all,

Had mixed their waters together,

But had not formed pastures, nor discovered reed-beds;

When yet no gods were manifest,

Nor names pronounced, nor destinies decreed,

Then gods were born within them." (Dalley 233)

"So you know the Sumerian's account of creation?" Helen inquired.

"This is the creation epic of Tlalocan not Oceanus." Galatea said.

"So it follows that the Sumerians were influenced by the Nagas and followed rituals to worship them as gods." Helen grasped the concept of aliens molding human civilization.

"Yes the Sumerians were among the first to be contacted by the Nagas and fell into their realm of influence but we will discuss this further tomorrow. Enjoy yourself for a new day in the Milky Way." Galatea gave the lesson of the day.

Powers, Brian, Phineas, Paulina, Helen, Rory and Belinda were among the crew who boarded *Calypso* in a shared hope to rescue Maia. Training had begun for the new recruits after they became accustomed to living aboard a starship.

"First we will do exercises to limber up and then you can swim in the pool. After that you can relax in the garden, enjoy snack time and then pause for meditation." Galatea was a health instructor.

So this is training...Powers thought he supposed it would involve military drills, pushups, climbing, and other strenuous exercise.

"Relax hurtful feelings, let go of selfishness, jealousy, hatred, and animosity. Focus yourself on the One, the source of your being." Galatea coached.

On board the Nishi Cruiser *Tangaroa*, Commander Ulani was preparing a plan of battle with the Admiralty. All civilians and Guard soldiers were given leave of the vessel, for this mission would be a dangerous one. Spoon and his squad of veteran fighters bid goodbye to the Nishi, and Ulani was given command of first attack on the moon base.

An unexpected event occurred in Eastern Europe. A large unidentified vessel was detected on Coalition radar in the midst of a battle against Naga positions. Turkish jets were targeting a Naga base when their squadron was attacked by a UFO. Witnesses on the ground were watching the jets coming in low for strafing runs when suddenly a very large, jagged vessel. It looked as if it was made of chards of ice assembled in triangular patterns but very black and dark.

Turkish pilots attacked the vessel after it did not respond to friendly codes, and shot missiles into its side. The missiles exploded upon impact but had little effect other than the surface of the ship glowed and quickly absorbed the energy. Then a series of bursts with blue tracers targeted the jets. Within moments all jets were hit and fell out of control to the ground, exploding on impact. The stealthy vessel disappeared quickly from the scene but not before being captured on video camera.

This was a disaster for Coalition forces as the Nagas advanced into Turkish territory. Nishi command assessed the Turkish squadron aircraft armor to be nanotube fullerene capable of absorbing and attenuating cosmic ray bursts into a super conductive field, but these bursts were of a much greater intensity than those of the Dragon ships. After viewing the video it was clear that the strange vessel was a Xibalban warship. This incident called for all Nishi commanders to be present for a conference on how to deal with this nemesis from the black hole sun.

Generations ago the Xibalbans entered the Nishi home solar system but not before being detected by friendly forces in the galaxy. The Nishi had prior knowledge of the depredations of Xibalban pirates within the galaxy, preparations were made to protect their world with a force field as well as their ships. Nishi technicians invented a fullerene shield for their craft using a carbon 60 configuration. This shield would be the test against the gamma ray bursts of the Xibalban pirates.

At the beginning of the battle a few Xibalban vessels broke through the force field surrounding the planet. Then the battle for the life of the people began. Xibalban pirates swooping down on the villages were met by Nishi warships. Most of the Nishi people were underground and protected from the pirates. Only the natural world remained above but even these defenseless creatures the pirates destroyed. Nishi warriors intercepted the Xibalban fire and withstood the onslaught. The fullerene shield absorbed the Xibalban fire completely and rerouted the energy into a weapon that brought the pirate ships down in disgrace. Thousands of pirates were captured, interrogated and then fed to hungry volcanoes. It was only fair to send them to their fiery home.

Now, the Nishi faced a new threat, how to protect a world that was not prepared to fight such a foe. It was not known how many Xibalban vessels were located outside the protective zone of the heliosphere. More puzzling was how a Xibalban vessel slipped through the Nishi guard posts. Xibalban pirates may have established a secret base in the solar system before the arrival of the Nishi fleet. All aircraft would have to be recalled and retrofitted with C60 armor. Otherwise the battle would be lost when the Xibalban pirates return in their hit and run tactics.

Federation agents of US Command interrogated the Naga Commander Budi after his surrender following his defeat at the battle of Brunswick. Budi threw them a bone to distract his foes. He did not care for Wangee, his mate and mother of his children on distant Tlalocan. He felt her disdain of him and his warlike ways. Wangee was a daughter of a Neyalan chieftain who promised her to Budi to make peace between the clans. She reluctantly joined with Budi and had regretted. Coming to Oceanus with Budi, she had to leave her children behind with her family in Tlalocan. Wangee liked her new world and its enchanting name. The moon loomed large in her dreams even brighter than Wulan, the moon over Tlalocan. Helios was brighter than the three stars that illuminated her home planet. Nights were darker without the moon on Oceanus unlike her nights on Tlalocan. Her people the Neyalan were peaceful and did not approve of the aristocracy and their wars of aggression and greed. She was a strong sensual female but very delicate in her movements like a dancer on a stage.

Federal agents surrounded the hideout, an old historic homestead situated along the old Raritan canal. An ancient dwelling built before the Revolution of '76, it was restored recently before the Invasion. The agents disabled three Naga guards and entered the house. Wangee was stunned at the sudden arrival of men in fatigues with weapons drawn. Afraid she might be hurt, she put away her knitting, a hobby she was learning to pass the time and stood still. An agent spoke out and told the others to stand down.

"Hello madam. We are not here to hurt you but rescue you from harm. Xibalbans are on the loose and could take you prisoner." Private Tom reached out to her.

"Oh, thank Wulan. Take me away from here!" Wangee cried out.

"Come with us. We will bring you to a safe haven. My name is Tom."

"Hello Tom. I will go with you freely. I have no weapons concealed not even these knitting needles." Wangee giggled.

"Ok it is our policy to frisk strangers, so please cooperate." Tom informed her.

"Oh, please do. I don't mind being frisked by handsome men." Wangee grinned widely. The men could not suppress wide smiles, for her beauty astonished them.

Wangee hated the Xibalbans. She remembered as a child a time when the horrible Xibalbans came to her village near the sea. She was playing with friends under the shade of a large Monkeepuzzle tree. A chief, who was known for his outspoken views against Xibalban aggression, was visiting. Xibalban thugs found this chief and executed him in public as a lesson to the resistance. She thought they were the ugliest creatures she had ever seen. She pictured them now as upright Komodo Dragons with stubby tails but uglier. There was not a grain of goodness in any of them. They were a race of the damned, damned to eternal damnation, a nest of vipers devoted to the black hole sun. Here she was a Naga being befriended by humans from Oceanus. Maybe there was hope after all for her people.

She told the Federal agents all she knew about the Xibalbans. Also she related what her lover Valentin had heard of a plan of the Xibalbans to invade Tlalocan and recapture the Geledek. It was a weapon of immense power that could magnify signal strength and bring the power of lightning to the bearer. If the Xibalbans acquired Geledek, they could employ it to amplify their cosmic blasters and defeat the Nishi.

At this very moment the Xibalbans were laying siege to Chicago. The reptilians looted jewelry stores and were wearing ill-gotten necklaces and gems around their thick necks like bling bling. They did not like the food of humans but relished eating humans raw or roasting them over a fire pit. The strange habits of Xibalbans puzzled humans. They would surge into battle without armor relying on firepower and terror to strike fear into the minds of the populace. Unlike the Nagas, they did not entice humans into coming into their sinister fold of pirates. Their leader was known as Croc by the humans. The troops called him a crock of shit.

Croc began the offensive in late summer and within a few weeks had seized the southern half of the city. Then the advance stalled. Croc was shocked at the ferocity of the Chicagoans. At first the humans ran in terror from his minions eating the people who fell into their grasp, but then the humans fought back with a vengeance shooting down his fierce draconian troops in droves.

Now, it was November and cold and windy in Chicago. The Xibalbans had lost their drive and sought shelter from the cold in the shadows. The Guard flushed them out with water cannons, smoke bombs and grenades then gunned them down mercilessly. Within weeks the battle was lost and the Xibalbans were in retreat looking for a ship to rescue them from this prison of cold. They had been badly defeated and now faced an air war with the Nishi.

The Naga command was flustered with the sudden onset of the Xibalbans. In Eastern Europe and the Middle East, K'ny mercenaries deserted by the thousands. Two young K'ny soldiers on the front advancing into Bulgaria witnessed the atrocities of Naga aggression. The river valley of Maritsa reminded them of home, but the blooming flowers outshone their memories. The people reminded them of their ancestors on Tlalocan. Balder and Bahram were tired of fighting and, tired of seeing the agony and distress of people who reminded them of their families at home. After a terrible battle on the plains of Ukraine, Balder rose out of the smoke filled ruins of towns. He saw bodies strewn on the blood soaked field of gore as a vulture soared overhead. He found his friend brave Bahadur lying on top of the foe with a sword in his hand. The man beside him was no K'ny soldier but his features were like his kin. He stopped to look at other faces...so familiar.

How could it be? He pondered. Have we killed our own people? Such thoughts echoed in his mind. He stumbled along, wondering what had gone wrong, why so many of the foe looked like his K'ny kin. Through the gloom the sun set like a fire in the forest denuded with the smell of death lingering. He hid in base camp with a few of his comrades still alive.

He asked Bahram "How many of the one hundred twenty are left?"

"Just eleven, my friend, the rest are dead." Bahram replied sadly.

"Have we killed our own? So many of the faces look like K'ny." Balder complained.

"Don't you know, brother? These are our kin from long ago. We have killed our brothers and sisters and they have killed us." Bahram lamented.

"What should we do? Go on killing?" Balder asked for advice.

"I've had enough. I'm quitting this mess. To hell with the Nagas! They left us here to die." Bahram said.

"If I had known I would not have fought this battle. But what will we do now? They will kill us after what we have done." Balder was despondent.

"We could surrender." Bahram suggested.

"Surrender?" Balder figured Bahram wasn't talking sense.

"Maybe we could switch sides." Bahram went a step further.

A woman invited them into her home, gave them food and hospitality, mended their wounds and spoke to them with words of kindness. There were pictures hanging on the wall of the kitchen of Mary and her son. Her son was on the cross bleeding from his wounds. Balder wondered if the dying man was her son, and he was a guest in her home. He felt guilty. Never did he or his comrade subject any person to this kind of torture, yet as a K'ny mercenary, he felt he was making these gentle people vulnerable to Naga persecution. Bahram felt the pang of guilt as well.

"Who is that man on the cross?" Bahram asked Bogomila, lady of the house.

"Isus, the one who died for us." Bogomila answered in her mother tongue.

Balder and Bahram were puzzled. Bogomila understood their blindness.

"He died that we may live." Bogomila spoke gently.

"Was he your son?" Balder wondered.

"He was the son of God." Bogomila humbly stated.

"What god would let his son die on a cross of shame?" Bahram figured the woman to be a fool.

Bogomila's eyes shined with joy. "There was no shame in his death. The Creator of the universe let his son die as a sacrifice."

"Why did not the Creator just kill his foes with thunder and lightning?" Balder was puzzled by this concept. She worshipped a man who died a shameful death. He was no hero.

"The Creator loves you and all of his creation" Bogomila said tenderly.

They were dumfounded by her answers.

"Why would the Creator sacrifice his own son? It makes no sense why a father would let his son die at the hands of his foes." Balder was very direct.

"Jesus conquered Death in his sacrifice to save his friends. He was given power to rise from death as the firstborn of heaven and Captain of the heavenly hosts. He sits on the right hand of his father on the throne in glory." Bogomila's voice rose in joy and power as it reached into the hearts of the young men before her.

A wave of light blazed into the minds of Bahram and Balder. Their eyes rested on a picture of Mary.

"Who is the beautiful lady?" Bahram thought it might be Astarte.

Bogomila looked at her guests with eyes that pierced their souls. "Her name is Maria. She gave birth to Jesus from the spirit of the Creator."

"You mean the Creator gave his spirit to Maria and Jesus was part of him? Balder questioned skeptically.

"Yes. The Creator gives his spirit through his son and everyone who believes in him." Bogomila explained.

"Wow! How can I have the spirit you speak of?" Bahram pleaded.

"When you believe, the Spirit will live in you." Bogomila spoke joyfully.

"Can you show me?" Balder implored.

"You must relinquish your old ways and learn the ways of the son." Bogomila said softly.

They were hooked line and sinker and left their weapons in Bogomila's house and followed her to a refuge for believers and deserters from the army of desolation.

On board the Nishi starship *Calypso*, Powers was attending yoga lessons and learning to meditate on the oneness of creation. The gardens of the *Calypso* were delightful with plenty of fresh fruit to pick and enjoy especially with his favorite girl by his side.

"Slap me! Am I awake, Powers? This is some kind of dream in this space odyssey. Just look at you and me here in paradise." Helen's eyes dazzled in the light filtering from the shade of trees, Powers looked into her eyes of blue and kissed her lips gently.

"Oh Will I am dreaming just keep it coming." Helen sighs, kissing him with passion, wrapping her arms around him.

"Honey, we have gone through the Gateway of Scorpio." Powers whispered.

"You mean the constellation of Scorpio?" Helen asked.

"Yes. It is a guidepost from a point near Oceanus to this distant star system." Powers elaborated.

"I read somewhere that the sting of the Scorpion killed Orion the hunter." Helen showed off her literacy.

Powers challenged her. "Do you know the star which is the heart of the Scorpion?"

"Antares the red star is also called the Stinger." Helen stated.

"Your knowledge of the heavens impresses me. However we are nowhere close to this giant star. We are approaching the star RA which shines on Tlalocan." Powers replied.

"So the dream is ending. We will have to confront our enemies the Naga on that inhospitable planet." Helen grumbled.

"Yes. As you well know we have been preparing for a spy mission these past few months." Powers reminded her.

"You could leave that to Valentin, master spy who fooled you with his friend Tatiana." Helen retorted.

"That is not for me to decide. I can understand your reticence regarding her." Powers defended his honor.

"Our mission is to rescue Maia from her captors and steal the Geledek." Powers reiterated the mission.

Tired of fighting, Helen said. "I don't know where I fit in with these ambitious plans."

"Maybe you should talk with Galatea. Your service here is voluntary." Powers thought she needed counsel.

The *Calypso* made its final approach toward the RA star system encompassing the planet Tlalocan. Admiral Mitsuo sent the strike force team in a pod on their assigned mission to retrieve the Geledek and rescue Maia. Geledek was an angelic sword given to the forerunner of the Xibalbans who turned rogue after the sun that shined on their world turned cold. Now, it was in the possession of the Naga aristocracy who did not know of its ultimate power.

Maia was destined to be the mother of a new race of people within this star system, but for now she was lost on a lonely planet. She was enraged with the molesting pirates who captured her and were taking her to god knows where.

Deceived into believing she was being raptured and saved from a world in desolation, she soon discovered that her deliverers were no angels but demons in disguise. Her cruel captors subjected her to rape and depravity. Upon her arrival on Tlalocan she was imprisoned in a domicile close to the palace for the Emperor's pleasure.

After three days of agonizing fear and anxiety, she made her escape, by stabbing two guards. She felt the pursuit of hostile Nagas through the savannah but evaded them running into the cover of the jungle. Her heart pounding she felt a power inside pulsing as if she could overpower her adversaries. After her run, she recalled jumping over boulders and streams with ease.

Strange figures appeared behind trees in the forest holding spears. She was surrounded but felt no fear as if she was invincible. Standing up she held onto a sword she had stolen from a guard and gazed into the eyes of the forest creatures. An older one made a sign with a finger and the others lowered their spears. He then uttered in a tongue Maia somehow understood as saying "Come be our guest." These creatures had faces similar to Nagas but were covered with colorful feathers.

As she was walking along, birdlike flying reptiles glided past her and landed on nearby trees to get a look at her. The entire forest seemed to be gazing at her. The forest was dark and deep with beams of light shining through in few places where large trees had fallen. Maia liked the mossy like undergrowth. She noticed furry creatures like rodents scurrying about among fallen trees and hollowed logs.

Crossing a stream she washed her hands in the rippling water and was astonished that her nails were glowing blue. She wondered if it was the water. Her forest companions looked at her with reverence and bent down to show their fealty to her. She did not understand what they wanted from her but followed them to their village. On entering a clearing a tribe of people young to old greeted her and bowed down to her in reverence. Maia was gracious and gave her hand in friendship to each of them. Beaming from ear to ear, they accepted her grace with smiles and shouts of joy.

Children led her in a procession of dance with accompanying drums and flutes. In a circle the children danced around her and led her to a hut decorated with bow of flowers. They sang a song of the Queen of the Forest and took her inside a hut where she could rest. Older children brought wooden trays of fruit and nuts for their Queen, for Maia had fulfilled the prophecy of a lady bathed in blue light who would deliver them from Naga aggression. In the hut Maia could now see a blue light around her even in the dark of night. She could not comprehend its meaning but an inner peace came upon her as she rested with the forest people known as the Hutan.

Maia felt a heightened level in all in her senses. She could understand the tongue of the Hutan and even the language of the birds. The birds flying in the forest were colorful but unlike any on Oceanus. The Hutan were feathery like birds but human like in physique and intelligence. Maia thought the Hutan were an example of convergent evolution but an idea sparked in her mind that a cosmic code brought about this evolution. An elder Hutan, Kurun spoke to her about the Naga race.

"The Naga race once lived among us many thousands of years ago. During the time of many fires, the light foot Naga left the forest to live in the grasslands beyond the great forest. The Nagas learned to fly on the Dragons who were our enemies. Since that time the Nagas forsook their forest home and took to the air with their Dragon allies. Together, the Nagas and Dragon pairs harassed the mighty Allosaurs and fought the monsters for ages in a death struggle. We Hutan were against fighting the Allosaurs. We suffered after each battle as the Allosaurs assaulted us in our forest home in a rampage after the Naga stole their eggs. Our homes were destroyed, and there were few places to hide. In the end, the Naga defeated the Allosaurs driving them into extinction but at great cost to the Hutan. Since the time of the Fire, the Naga rarely visit the forest, and the Hutan never visit the Naga overlords."

"Why have you become so estranged?" Maia asked.

"The Naga have become like Allosaurs, arrogant and belligerent." Kurun explained.

"The Hutan never venture outside their forest home?" Maia was curious about Hutan behavior.

"We Hutan do have occasions to visit the Neyalan and trade with them." Kurun disclosed.

"So you have no visitors other than the Neyalan?" asked Maia.

"There is a strange tribe called the Riskani who roam the forest like rangers. One came to visit us recently. He was looking for a blue-eyed lady with long black hair." Kurun smiled.

"What was his name?" Maia inquired.

Kurun grinned. "Koko."

"Aren't you the clever one! Are you holding me for ransom?" Maia had heard about the rascal Koko.

"Oh no. The Hutan believe you are the Queen of the Forest, here to deliver us from the Naga." Kurun returned to his original tack.

Maia thought about this for a moment. There could be an opportunity for her to hide and escape from the Naga.

"What would you have me do?" Maia hoped the Hutan could protect her.

"Use your powers to overcome the Naga and set us free to once again roam all of Pataloka." Kurun declared.

"Pataloka is the name of your world, this planet?" Maia stammered.

"It is the name we have heard from the sacred texts in the beginning when TopaNaga begat us from the sea." Kurun proclaimed proudly.

"Who is TopaNaga?" Maia was perplexed at this new creature maybe a monster.

"She is the Dragon of the western sea." Kurun said.

"I suppose that was in ancient times." Maia thought she had encountered a primitive people immersed in myth.

"We Hutan dream of a time to come when a lady of your bearing will deliver us and set us free to roam the savannah and not be harassed by the Naga and their pet Dragons." Kurun expressed the Hutan belief in a deliverer.

Maia saw an opportunity to rest and hid from her captors. "Very well but I must rest until the setting of the two moons."

Maia strolled over to her hut to rest. She noticed the hut glowed green. She entered and saw to her amazement a swirl of sparkling dust like pollen from a pine. She soon fell asleep and dreamed of a world transformed into paradise.

What Kurun did not tell Maia was that the Hutan were a symbiotic race with the forest fungi living in the soil. When a Hutan person died, they were laid to rest in a special hut. Fungi in the soil would inhabit the body and absorb the soul of the Hutan who died. The family of the Hutan would choose a pregnant woman or a lost soul to rest in the hut. Overnight the fungi spores would transmit the consciousness of the departed person into the fetus or the lost person. In this way, the soul of a person could live on for generations.

In the morning Maia awoke with a new consciousness born of the Hutan but with a memory of her recent self as well.

Maia looked into the sky and saw a large craft speeding through the clouds. Her heart skipped a beat, she wondered if her captors were scanning her position from above.

Upon releasing the strike force, Admiral Mitsuo discovered a Naga starship orbiting the Tlalocan. A vessel launched from the starship on a heading to land on the planet.

"Sire, there is an unidentified vessel entering the RA system and heading toward Tlalocan." Lieutenant Toshiaki reported.

"Zoom in on the vessel to identify and bring it on screen Lieutenant." Admiral Mitsuo ordered.

"Aye, Aye Sire." Lieutenant Toshiaki replied.

A huge vessel appeared on screen with a jagged profile.

"Undoubtedly this is a Xibalban vessel." Admiral Mitsuo issued a command. "All decks Battle Stations Ready, Alert All Battle Stations."

Admiral Mitsuo decided to send an additional escort of warriors to protect the Strike force. Cyrene, a Nephali was chosen to lead the expedition. Koko piloted the star fighter bearing the Strike force toward the eastern shore of the Northern Sea and landed near a village. The vessel landed safely in a cleared area of sand behind the cover of tall trees. The party of seven disembarked, hid the craft with boughs of tree limbs and headed east toward a village by the shore. Rory alerted the team to an aircraft racing over the sea and getting larger as it zoomed toward their position.

"Wow, that was a close one!" Belinda uttered.

"Good thing we covered our vessel! That looked like a Xibalban vessel." Powers exclaimed.

"It will be getting dark soon. We must keep going to reach the village." Koko pointed out.

Just after sunset the party reached the outskirts of the village. An elder approached them in the light of two moons.

"Koko, it has been many moons my friend!" Dukun raised his arms to greet his friend.

"Dukun, you look well! How is your family, my friend?" Koko raised his arms with palms outward to show friendship.

"They are well. What brings you here with these I do not know?" Dukun was leery of the strangers in Koko's company.

"We have come to beseech your chief on behalf of your daughter, Wangee." Koko appealed to the Neyalan elder.

"Oh is my daughter hurt?" Dukun was deeply concerned.

Koko calmed his fears. "No she is well and in the care of the Nishi who are protecting her from the Xibalbans."

"My daughter is safe then?" Dukun was not so sure of the Nishi.

"Yes." Koko assured him. "Our last transmission stated she was in protective custody on Oceanus."

"When is she returning home? Has her husband been captured?" Dukun presses Koko further.

"Her husband was captured and is being held by the humans on Oceanus. He is considered a war criminal. I do not know when Wangee can return." Koko replied.

"I am not surprised to hear the fate of Budi. He was an arrogant fool bragging he would conquer another world. Let me take you to the chief." Dukun detested Budi.

"Oh my god! What was that flying overhead?" Paulina was frightened.

"Naga terbang. What you would call a Dragon." Dukun knew the tongue of Oceanus quite well.

"I have seen these fire breathing Dragons that the Nagas use in battle." Helen commented.

"They have to be trained to breathe fire. These will not hurt you." Dukun reassured Paulina.

"Good to know a good Dragon from a bad one." Paulina was being sarcastic.

Dukun chuckled. "Yes. We have only friendly Dragons in Neyalan lands."

"We have heard the Neyalan fisher folk are different from the Naga and K'ny warmongers." Helen said to her host.

Yes, indeed. We Neyalan are proud of our heritage. We do not believe in waging war except in self-defense." Dukun replied.

"Do not the Naga fight against you and try to conquer you and your lands?" Helen inquired.

"It is not in the nature of Nagas to fight amongst themselves. But recently the aristocracy has been stirring up troubles." Dukun admitted.

"Can you tell me more about these troubles?" Helen pried.

"When Wangee was a child, Xibalbans came to our village and arrested a rebel chief. They tortured and mutilated him publicly before killing him. The Nagas stood by and did nothing." Dukun would not defend the Nagas.

"Has more trouble erupted since then?" Helen inquired.

"Plenty. The villages erupted in force rampaged through Naga lands and drove off the Xibalbans. Anapa the Emperor abandoned his throne and Biru became lord of the Naga. He vowed to protect all the Hutans and Neyalans." Dukun expounded.

"Did he make good on his pledge?" Helen asked.

"No, he is a trickster. We discovered he was dealing with the Xibalbans for profits in piracy." Dukun indicted Biru.

They reached the hut of the chief and Dukun introduced his new found friends. "Chief, we have some visitors. Koko has brought them."

Chief Jago was wary of Koko. "Hmmm Koko, have you brought me trouble, Riskani?"

"Not that you don't have trouble already! We have seen a Xibalban vessel fly overhead." Koko informed the Chief.

"I would like to get rid of that pirate scum and send them to hell!" Jago was enraged over the Xibalbans.

"We have a plan to defeat them but first we have a present for you and the people of your village." Koko turned to Rory and asked, "Could you present the chief with our gift?"

Rory gave Chief Jago a box.

"Oh thank you." the chief said and opened the box.

"This is very generous of you. We Nelayan love chocolate! If only we could grow the beans here!" Jago was grateful.

"Maybe someday when there is peace with Oceanus." Helen suggested.

Jago agreed. "Yes that would be wonderful to have friends to trade with across the galaxy."

On board the *Calypso*, Powers had time to ponder a vision of life on Oceanus. No more war. The pirates were vanquished and nature in all its glory was restored. People lived in villages. There were no more cities spread across the continents. No more monolithic buildings to hide the sun. Villages were clusters of neighborhoods wherein everyone knew each other. The human world was divided into regions according to culture. These regions were sovereign and ruled by people who held elections to choose leaders worthy to uphold their culture and economy. A central government was ruled by a council of elders. This council of Oceanus was advised by the Galactic Federation which included the Nishi.

Throughout Oceanus the economy was based on the conservation of natural resources. All people lived in neighborhoods in multi-family housing with the exception of a few who were allowed to live as hermits for spiritual enlightenment or scientific endeavors. Housing was designed exclusively as active or passive solar unless other, like geothermal was more efficient. Most people lived above ground and travelled by a network of rails in tubes suspended above the landscape, locally by foot or bicycle or by boat in water ways and sea.

Fossil fuel use was restricted to underground factory work. A minority of people chose to work and live underground. All factories, shopping malls and retro living was done underground and not allowed above.

Above ground, villages were connected to a network of parks open to wildlife. Villages were enclosed to protect wildlife but wildlife parks were open without any fences so the buffalo could once again roam free with the wolves. There were no roads, cars, trucks, trains or highways to interrupt the ecosystem of Oceanus. Farms and gardens were enclosed within villages. Streams and lakes were tended as nurseries to nurture a healthy food web for fishes, birds, amphibians, reptiles, mammals and all creatures big and small. For streams flowed into estuaries, that were the nurseries of the seas of Oceanus and all its wonderful life in the sea. Tiny phytoplankton formed the base of a food web that fed the zooplankton, fish, and mighty whales. It was from these tiny creatures that life evolved from a sulfurous atmosphere to a fresh sea breeze wind full of oxygen for humans to breathe. Of course, all the plants especially the forests played their part in keeping the climate healthy for humans and wildlife.

During the days of Desolation, wars against nature and humanity raged for thousands of years. It was during this time that evil people infected with ignorance and greed stripped the land of forests and even the grass of the prairies to mine the land and sea for minerals, urban developments or factory farming. In the hell that was to follow with trade wars and religious fanaticism, the ecosystems of Oceanus began to plummet and be overturned. With all the debris of organic matter and pollution going through rivers into the seas, anoxic regions along the continental shelves rapidly grew and fish populations disappeared. Atomic bomb testing by maniacal world powers destroyed the ecological balance of the seas. Heterotrophic bacteria in the seas and land proliferated and overturned the food web. Forests were disappearing from the land and phytoplankton populations were shrinking to low levels.

Humanity was on the brink of extinction with the rise of bacteria that released carbon dioxide and sulfur dioxide. The rise of Pre-Cambrian sulfur bacteria would be the next step after the seas became wastelands. But a miracle occurred which averted this disaster. It came from a blast like trumpet, a starburst that sent the foe reeling in defeat.

The remains of roads were used for bicycling and hikers enjoying the wonders of nature. People travelled by tube tunnels erected above the landscape to get from village to village. There was also shuttle traffic by air and tube transit under the seas.

Children were taught the importance of the diversity of life and the ever pressing need to preserve species. Teachers took children outdoors to observe wildlife in the natural world throughout Oceanus. It was primary for children to learn their place in the world among all the creatures of Oceanus of which they were one. In this way the wolf, mountain lion, eagle and grizzly were free once more to roam on the happy hunting grounds with plentiful herds of deer, antelope, bison and elk. Rivers ran free with pristine water full of insect larvae to feed a bountiful supply of fish. Estuaries and wetlands were restored. Oil tankers no longer transported their sludge of oil across the precious seas spilling the toxic oil into the water and spoiling the home of porpoises and whales. Anoxic regions were confined to the deepest regions of deep sea volcanic vents and crevices. Phytoplankton thrived in large blooms in swirls rivaling the rainforests in productivity. The mighty whales once again ruled the seven seas.

In his reverie Powers was listening to a favorite song of the Nishi, "Yoshi no mi."

"There is a faraway island, I don't know the name.

From this island came a coconut floating on the ocean.

How long have you, coconut, been drifting on the waves,

so far from the coast of your home?"

In the vastness of space, Powers felt like a coconut drifting and looking for his home. Little did he know his home was threatened at this very moment with annihilation from a nihilistic foe devoted to their cult of the Black hole sun.

Commander Ulani at the helm of the *Tangaroa* was pursuing a squadron of Xibalban vessels intent on landing at their secret Moon base. He was not alone. Another five Nishi starships were in pursuit following the *Tangaroa* to intercept and destroy the Xibalbans and their base of operations.

"Tangaroa! Commander Tamihana of the *Rangatira* calling." Was the transmission heard on the bridge of the *Tangaroa*.

"Yes, we hear you Commander." Ulani confirmed.

"We are under attack by a Xibalban vessel. Request permission to engage enemy." Commander Tamihana replied urgently

"Fire at once, Commander." Ulani ordered. "We are behind you."

Commander Tamihana directed fire at the Xibalban vessel. The Xibalbans returned fire at the *Ringatira*, rocking the Nishi starship.

"Lieutenant Ryota, assess battle damage." Tamihana ordered.

"The hull has not been breached. Weapon systems operable, Sire." Lieutenant Ryota reported.

"Fire on the Xibalbans!" Tamihana ordered.

A blue light, like a lightning strike into the foe, shot from the bow of the *Ringatira*. The jagged hulk of the pirate vessel folded as the hull was breached in a blaze of fire. In the midst of the debris field, a myriad of ships suddenly appeared, their jagged shapes uncloaked in the darkness of space. Tamihana was stunned by the vision on screen, hundreds of Xibalban vessels surrounded his ship.

"Fire at the ship directly in front of our bow!" Tamihana ordered courageously.

Tamihana got off one shot but a melee of blasts struck the *Ringatira* from all sides. The hull was breached and all were lost in a moment.

Not able to engage the foe. Ulani witnessed the battle from a distance.

"All fleet commanders, prepare to face the enemy in one final battle. We must protect Oceanus!" Ulani was determined to fight on.

Ulani understood the odds against so many Xibalbans, but he would not flee the scene of battle. Ulani led the fleet in a chevron formation toward the foe.

Out of the darkness of space a great light shot from a distant star. Its aim was true. Ulani saw the light coming from afar.

"Nishi Commanders follow me and live another day." Ulani ordered.

Ulani swerved to the right and turned his squadron of ships in retreat. The Xibalbans stayed for a while in position before giving chase. The pulse of light lit up the Xibalban fleet of a thousand ships for a moment. Then they were gone. Tamihana's sacrifice had not been in vain. AO answered his prayer. What was once a mighty empire of pirates was vanquished by a pulsar.

Awaking from his dream, Powers spoke.

"Yes how wonderful it would be to trade beans across the galaxy!" He said in his reverie.

"Wait until you taste the sweetness of our smoke here." Dukun offered Powers a puff of the cigar he was smoking.

"Smells familiar, like the cannabis we grow in the Sierra Foothills." Powers reminisced.

"Some time ago we were given a batch of seeds by no other than Koko. The seeds germinated in our moist soil by the sea and grew to the size of small trees." Dukun bragged.

"Potent stuff! I like the taste. What do you call your brand?" Powers was exhilarated.

"Koko calls it 'skunk weed'. So I suppose we will go with that." Dukun joked.

"You've got to come up with a better brand my friend if you want to be successful in marketing. Skunks are known for their innocuous odor." Powers set him straight.

"What do you suggest? We know little of your culture. What is a skunk?" Dukun was curious.

"A skunk is a small mammal that has black hair, a tail, walks on four legs and has a white stripe down it's back. If you threaten a skunk, it will spray you with an obnoxious odor which will persist for days. None of your lady friends or anyone will come near you." Powers chuckled.

"That is curious to hear. I was hoping to draw more of the ladies by smoking this weed." Dukun was disappointed to hear about 'skunk weed'.

"Has it worked?" Powers was dubious.

"Only in my dreams." Dukun smiled.

"Rest assured, my friend, we could work out a deal for you and trade beans for your weed." Powers offered to help.

"Ah, that is very good of you. Let us talk more of this over dinner. Please be seated by our table as our guest." Dukun showed his hospitality.

After dinner, Jago, chief of the Neyalans spoke to his visitors about the nature of their visit.

"Why have you come to our village when the Nishi are your allies?" Jago was wary of the strangers' intentions.

"We are from Oceanus, a planet far away. Our people are besieged by the Nagas and Xibalbans. We have heard that you fought the Xibalbans and drove them from your land." Powers explained.

"That is true. We did fight the Xibalbans and beat them. But why would you come here for our help?" Jago was not convinced.

"The Naga aristocracy has a weapon that can defeat the Xibalbans. We ask your help in getting it from them." Powers had a plan.

"I know of no such weapon unless you mean the Geledek. It is in the museum by the palace. There is a legend that Guntur wielded it to slay the sea Dragon." Jago was not easily fooled.

"That is the very weapon. The Nagas do not know its true power. However the Xibalbans are here and preparing to attack the citadel to steal the Geledek." Powers pointed out the danger to the Neyalans.

'What would the Xibalbans do with this artifact if they did steal it?" Jago doubted an ancient artifact could be a dangerous weapon.

"The Geledek is an ancient weapon that can magnify the power of a beam of electromagnetic energy or cosmic blast." Powers explained the nature of the artifact.

"Yes, I am familiar with the story of how Guntur brought forth lightning from the sky with this weapon!

I do not understand how he could do such a marvelous thing." Jago remarked.

"Jago! Are you with us? Will you help us defeat the Xibalbans before they get the Geledek?" Koko attempted to sway the chief.

"You are an anxious fellow Koko. We Neyalans prefer to think on these things for a while and not be hasty." Jago thought Koko was impetuous.

"Jago did you not see the Xibalban ship fly overhead?" Koko was incredulous at Jago's hesitation.

"Yes, indeed, I did but they did not land." Jago asserted.

"Are you going to wait until they steal the Geledek and blast your village to dust?" Koko said.

Jago stood steadfast in front of Koko for a few moments.

"I will discuss this matter with the village elders." Jago stated flatly and walked back to his hut.

Darkness crept into the village, but Koko and his six companions could not sleep. They heard Jago and the elders arguing for hours. It seemed they had broken the peace of the quiet village. Overhead, they heard the passing of vessels that could be none other than Xibalban. They were massing for an assault. But would Jago understand this danger or think they had come as spies?

Jago erupted from his hut with a cadre of Neyalan warriors armed with spears. He came toward the seven interlopers with an intense stare.

"We have decided to hear your plan." Jago spoke directly with Powers.

"Very well honored chief of the Neyalan people, we have not much time. The Xibalbans are gathering for an attack on the Naga citadel." Powers was eager to hear the chief.

"Let's hear it. We Neyalan want this Geledek to slay the Xibalbans." Jago was interested.

Powers laid out the plan Koko had drawn and detailed in the Neyalan script. Fires were lit to illuminate the map and strategy.

"I commend you, Koko. This is a good plan but you have left out one thing."

"What is that, chief?" Koko had an idea what he might say but waited.

"Who gets the Geledek after you steal it?" Jago asked slyly.

"It is yours to keep. But I must advise you, we are together in this battle to defeat the Xibalbans. To use this weapon against them, we must harness it to the transformer of the Nishi starship." Koko warned him.

"How do I know this weapon will be returned to us?" Jago challenged him.

"I have been your friend for all these years. The Nishi are here to defeat the Xibalbans. We have a common enemy who want to eradicate us." Koko put is his plan on the line.

"Very well, Koko. We will stand together to the end, my friend." Jago put his arm on Koko's shoulder.

Little did Powers and his companions realize that Jago had sentries posted all around the Neyalan territory and spies within the walls of the Naga citadel. Jago was well aware of the Xibalban presence already approaching the Naga stronghold.

"We Neyalans have a plan for your friends to enter the palace of Buku." Jago said.

Powers was puzzled. "I have showed you our plan. Do you not approve?"

"Your plan is bold, but I assure you, the Naga sentries will arrest you before you enter the palace." Jago revealed.

"What do suggest we do?" Powers asked for his advice.

"You are in need of disguises. We can make you look like natives and thereby gain entrance with an entourage of Neyalan seeking an audience with the Emperor." Jago explained more of his plan.

"That sounds like a great idea." Powers approved.

"Very well, bring all your companions together. We must be ready by morning light." Jago was now in charge.

Powers, Brian, Phineas, Paulina, Helen, Rory and Belinda were disguised as K'ny with distinct features notably dark complexion, dark hair and prominent noses. Paulina had a dark complexion with black hair but her nose was small so a mold was made to give her a beak. Phineas had a prominent beak but a fair complexion. Being a descendant of the Nishi people, Koko, a Riskani could transform his features at will.

RESCUE MISSION

In the early morning, the seven companions set out across the hills and plain toward the Naga city with an entourage of Neyalan on horseback. In the hills to the east of the Naga city were entrenchments of Neyalan artillery and hidden aircraft to intercept any Xibalban fighters. The troop of Neyalan with Koko and his companions in tow reached the walls of the Naga castle by dawn. No hostile Xibalbans were in sight. However ships were known to be roaming the region.

Dukun requested an audience with Biru.

"His majesty is expecting you. Please come in honorable Dukun, chief of the Neyalan." Guard at the gate replied respectfully.

The entire troop of Neyalan and their strange guests entered the castle through the gate. A retinue of

Naga servants greeted their guests and escorted them to the courtyard to relax and enjoy refreshments.

Helen remarked at the wonderful array of exotic fruit. "Some of these fruits look familiar. Yes, these are mangos, bananas and pineapples."

"Try this one." Koko offered her a spiny fruit.

"Hmmm...the odor is funky and it is full of spikes. What's it called?" Helen tweaked her nose.

"Durian, taste the flesh." Koko encouraged her.

"Tastes sweet. Now I like it." Helen was delighted.

"Actually none of these fruits are native here." Koko disclosed.

"It appears these fruits come from Indonesia." Powers remarked.

"Yes, the Nagas prefer Indonesian fare." Koko confirmed.

"How do they transport fresh fruit across the galaxy?" Helen inquired.

"Naga farmers bring fruit from the foothills by wheeled carts." Koko gave her a simple answer.

"Nagas grow fruits from Indonesia here?" Powers was astounded.

"Yes, they have orchards in the southeast where there is plenty of rain." Koko said.

"I thought the Nagas were a warlike people not farmers." Will thought this news was strange.

"Most Nagas work for a living just like the people of Oceanus." Koko provided a picture of everyday life of ordinary Naga people.

"Well, I'm glad to receive their hospitality. This fruit banquet is mouthwatering." Helen was gracious.

"So how did the Nagas get the seeds to grow the fruit?" Powers wondered.

"A long time ago, a Naga ship carried a bounty of seeds to Pataloka." Koko showed his knowledge of Naga history.

"Has anyone seen Paulina?" Powers suddenly recalled her absence.

"No, she disappeared just after we entered through the gates." Belinda remarked.

"That's strange. I wonder what she is up to." Powers believed she was a spy for the Nagas.

"Whatever she is scheming, she does not know our plan." Koko reassured his friends.

Booming shock waves rocked the palace walls. The guests shook off their glad reverie and looked out to see the danger. They rushed out of the courtyard and entered the hall leading from the entry gate. Rory carrying a sword longer than he was tall, rushed into the hall. His feet slipped on the shiny floor and he lost his grip on the sword. It whirled across the hall toward the guests. Sparks flew as its razor-sharp edge bit the adamantine floor. People crowded in the hall dashed to and fro to escape the blade. A woman with long black hair and dressed in a brown cloak stood firm, stopped the blade with her boot. She picked up the silver sword and raised it up pointing to the crown of the hall. Powers wondered who this beautiful woman with a disguise may be. Her face was covered in a bird mask.

Outside the walls of the city, Neyalan artillery launched projectiles into troop formations of Xibalbans surrounding the castle. The sun was setting behind the castle walls. Twilight opened the doors of darkness to hordes of rapacious reptilians. Nagas made preparations to repel the invaders. Rockets were fired at Xibalban ships approaching the citadel. A squadron of Naga fighters had engaged the Xibalbans to the east. They had not returned. All of them were presumed lost. Neyalan forces entrenched in hidden positions to the east were blasting Xibalban ground positions. A few Xibalban troops gained entry to the fortress on the west side.

As the mysterious woman raised the sword, a blue aura surrounded her. From the west a strong wind blew into the hall behind her. She stood firm in a wide stance as the sword glistened with a blue flame. Behind the crowd emerged a noisy bellowing and a foul pestilence. The people shuddered in fear. Xibalbans pushed aside people and grimaced at the sword bearer. Their spiny tails whipped as they stomped and poked with weapons ready to assault anyone in their way. One known as Kroc, cried out and pointed a weapon at the lady in blue. Kroc swung his tail and took aim at the lady with her sword raised. Without a word from her lips she lowered the sword and leveled it at the Xibalbans. The crowd of people rushed out of the hallway and into the courtyard.

A blast rocked the hall. A thunderbolt unleased from the Geledek decimated the Xibalbans reducing them to ashes. The lady in blue grimly pulled the sword back to her side.

Her mask had dissolved in the fury of the thunderclap revealing her face. She noticed a familiar face looking in from the courtyard. Her memory whirled in a sea of youthful adventures of a place faraway and long ago. She blinked and he was still there gazing at her. So long ago he was lost in a storm on her home planet Oceanus. How could he be here?

She took a step toward him. Was it a trick? Was he real? She remembered his name.

"Tim!" She called out to him.

He smiled. Still youthful with his blond hair and blue eyes, where had he been all this time? She wondered...could it really be him?

"Maia!" Tim cried out.

Her heart thumped. She felt weak, yet joyful at the thought that he had returned to her. Across a galaxy of stars, he had found her. She ran to him. Tim started to quicken his step toward her, but she was upon him in a moment. He embraced her in his arms. She held him with her left arm, her right arm still holding the sword. She would protect him at all costs. She would not let him go this time.

He looked into her blazing eyes. She looked into his eyes and kissed him. Instantly she was aware of everything he did when he was gone, all the places and people played in her mind like a movie. He had been looking for her for ages across space and time. He never gave up. She was overwhelmed by the strength of his love for her. Looking into his eyes she saw a ship sailing across the sea of Oceanus.

"Who is she? Do you know her?" Powers asked Koko

"She is Maia, the one we came to rescue from the Nagas." Koko revealed.

"That's strange because now she has the Geledek." Belinda remarked.

"I wonder what she is going to do with it besides slay Xibalbans." Helen was fearful of this new personage.

"Yes and how are we going to get the Geledek from her?" Brian concurred.

Koko tried to sooth their fears. "She is in a trance now. She doesn't yet know the extent of her powers."

"What do you mean? I thought she was just a girl kidnapped from church." Phineas was confused about the turn of events.

"You are correct, yet she is a Nephali. She has recently metamorphosized." Koko revealed Maia's spiritual nature.

"So, is she going to turn into a butterfly?" Belinda was thinking of physical nature.

"Once she comes of age, she will be able to change her appearance at will." Koko explained what he meant by her transformation.

"Wow, it seems the tables have turned for us. She has rescued us from the Xibalbans." Brian saw the reality of the situation.

"Who is that guy she is embracing just now?" Helen was curious of another stranger in their midst.

"He is a time traveler from Oceanus. His name is Timothy. He was lost in a storm in Oregon some years ago and went back in time to the Ice Ages." Koko digressed about another story.

"The Ice Ages...you must be joking. This is getting crazy!" Powers was overwhelmed by all this talk of metamorphosis and time travel.

"Time is relative to the pull of your Sun. He and his friend were pulled by a magnetic thread into a warp of time and space and sent back 15,000 years." Koko said.

"How did he get back to where we are now?" Brian was curious about Koko's theory as he understood it.

"Another solar storm brought him back to a familiar place but at a time slightly in the future from when he left. He missed her by a few days." Koko was somewhat brash as if he had been there himself.

"Wow that is really sad." Belinda felt pathos for his plight.

"Yet he heard that she was kidnapped and got on the first ship here, the *Calypso*. He has done what no man has ever accomplished, travelling across a galaxy of stars and thousands of years to find her." Koko kindled the true spirit of this time traveler.

"They are gone, vanished!" Belinda was astonished.

"She will go back to the forest with the Hutan." Koko said in a matter of fact tone.

Always inquisitive, Helen asked. "Who are the Hutan?"

"They are the people of the forest. There is a legend among them that a lady will come to rescue them from oppression. She is known as the Queen of the Forest." Koko gave her something to ponder.

"The Hutan are oppressed by the Naga?" Belinda was surprised to hear about this bit of news.

"Yes. The Naga aristocracy are encroaching upon their land and forcing Hutan to work in forced labor building ships." Koko told her of the troubles of the Hutan.

"Do the Hutan believe Maia is the Queen of the Forest?" Helen was interested in legends and myths.

"Yes and that is why they have come here in force. They have laid siege to the west side of the castle and taken Biru and his cohorts as prisoners." Koko said.

"So how are we going to get the Geledek now that Rory slipped up?" Belinda inquired but she was interrupted by fighting close by.

With the departure of Maia and the Hutans, fighting broke out inside the castle walls. Cyrene arrived with a troop of warriors from the Nishi starship. Koko was in contact with the force and coordinated an attack near Biru's quarters on the eastern side of the citadel. Koko led his team of seven without Paulina who was missing. They soon encountered gruesome scenes of carnage within the castle. Heads decapitated from bodies of Nagas and human captives were lying about. Half eaten limbs discarded by the Xibalbans lay in pools of blood. Around a turn in the walls shots were fired at Koko and his team.

Koko climbed a wall and took the Xibalbans by surprise, shooting them from the top of the wall three meters high. The Xibalbans could not climb well and were struck down before they could fire back.

Powers urged the others on behind him. A Xiblaban jumped from a hidden corner at Powers. Helen shot the creature down before it could sink its teeth into Will. Then another hideous Xibalban shot Helen in the leg from behind a counter. Brian opened fire at the creature with a blaster and cut it down. Rory shot another as it attempted to escape. Phineas and Belinda rescued Helen from the firefight and stopped the bleeding in her leg. Koko told them to take her back to medivac with Rory. Brian and Powers would go on ahead to reconnoiter with Cyrene. There was no time for farewell. Powers was on the lookout for more Xibalbans ready to come out of hiding.

The Xibalbans concentrated their attack on the forests west of the citadel. They fired incendiaries into the Hutan villages from their vessels in the clouds above. Terrified villagers fled their homes seeking shelter in caves and underground tunnels. Neyalans led by Dukun surrounded the citadel, killing all the Xibalbans and leaving no prisoners but Nagas. Cyrene and her party met the Neyalans in the citadel and joined forces to rescue captives. They found women locked behind doors in a large room beside Biru's quarters.

Powers entered the room with the Neyalan troops. He discovered Tatiana huddled with the other women hiding behind drapes of the harem. She was dressed in fine silks but disheartened by her harsh treatment. She looked at Powers in disbelief, shaking her head and thinking it was but a dream.

"Is that you Will?" Tatiana spoke, her head in a daze.

Surprised to see her, Powers answered. 'It is I. How did you come to be here on this distant planet?"

"I was kidnapped by those nasty Naga creatures and brought to this hell hole." Tatiana replied.

"I went to find you in Brunswick but your apartment was demolished." Powers felt on the defensive.

"Oh it was so horrible! Is it finally over? I am so glad to see you!" Tatiana hoped to win him over.

Will embraced her, and she held him tight.

"I'm so glad you are alive. We must evacuate you and the other ladies to a medical transport for treatment." Will began to remember his last day with her.

"Oh no, I don't want to leave you! I have been so despondent since the day you left." Tatiana felt him slipping away.

Will remembered how she had betrayed him but restrained himself from saying anything about it. Again, she poured out her charms, but she was disheveled and ashamed of her appearance.

"I am on a dangerous mission. You will not be safe here." Powers asserted himself.

"Please Will, I want to stay with you. Take me home." Tatiana pleaded.

"You must trust me. If you listen you will be able to go home." Powers took command.

"Why are you on this mission? Did you come here to save me?" Tatiana saw herself as the center of his attention.

"I never told you. I am a fighter pilot with the US Naval forces." Will revealed his identity.

"You, a fighter pilot? You must be joking." Tatiana mocked him.

"No joke, I was a weekend warrior these past few years. It has been a long weekend lately." Powers said.

"So, that's what you were up to instead of going to school." Tatiana's eyebrows lift up.

"Yes, but I could not tell you. It was a secret assignment." Will opened his jacket and showed her his Navy squadron's insignia.

"Wow, you are my hero now!" Tatiana attempted a comeback.

"OK, girl, let's get on that transport and out of danger." Powers would have none of it.

"Where will they take me? I am so tired of being thrown about." Tatiana whimpered.

"You will be visiting a Nishi starship. They are our friends." Powers tried to cheer her up.

"Oh I don't like the sound of that, Will." Tatiana complained.

"It's like being on a cruise ship. They have fine accommodations. They will take good care of you." Powers knew how much she liked to go on cruises.

"Did you sail on this ship?" Tatiana was apprehensive about starships.

"I have been on this very ship for months and enjoyed every minute of the experience. There is a beautiful greenhouse there with fruit and flowers." Powers really wanted to get rid of her.

"That sounds wonderful, Will" Tatiana replied, the imagery reminded her of the Caribbean.

"I will see you soon. Take care." Powers sent her off.

Will escorted Tatiana and the other ladies along with Brian to the awaiting transport outside the eastern gate of the citadel.

"Good bye, Tatiana." Powers held her in his arms.

"Good bye, Will." Tatiana kissed him

It seemed to Will, her demeanor had changed since her kidnapping and brutal treatment at the hands of the Naga. For once, she was truly grateful for Will helping her.

Phineas, Belinda and Rory joined the others on the transport. Their mission was complete, so Koko decide not to risk their lives in the dangerous fight about to enfold. Powers joined a Nishi squadron patrolling the skies above the citadel. Will longed to see his friend Helen but was torn between her and Tatiana. He hoped to resolve his feelings tomorrow.

Brian insisted on staying with Koko to find Maia and Koko needed his help. They joined another Nishi force led by Cyrene, who led the expedition into the forests of the Hutan to find Maia.

The Nishi starship hovering over the citadel protected the Neyalan from Xibalban attack. The pirate ships gathered over the forests and threatened to annihilate the Hutan if the Nishi attacked.

Cyrene led the expedition into the forest under the cover of night. They soon encountered Xibalban troops on the ground burning Hutan villages. Cyrene gave the command to engage the enemy and a fierce fight broke out. Koko and his team followed in the wake of the assault. At a village near a waterfall, they found Maia and a troop of Hutan hiding behind rocks for shelter. Maia recognized Koko from a party with a friend long ago on Oceanus. She was very surprised to see him for he was a known as a party loving surfer back then.

"Koko, what on earth are you doing here?" Maia was shocked to see him.

"We are here to help you." Koko declared.

"You are going to help me against these ghastly creatures?" Maia was dubious of his claim.

"I am Riskani. My people live here. This is my home." Koko emphasized his mission.

"Ok I have heard this from the Hutan, that you are a messenger." Maia conceded.

"He is a damn good pilot as well." Brian said.

"Maia, this is my friend, Brian." Koko introduced him to her.

"I am glad to meet you." Maia extended her hand.

Brian took it gently in his. "I am glad to meet you lady."

"We seem to be outnumbered." Maia looked around and assessed the situation.

"Help is on the way. Cyrene and her Nishi warriors are engaged fighting the Xilbabans on the ground." Koko said.

"Great but how do we engage the pirates firing at the Hutan villages?" Maia addressed the battle from the air.

Koko shifted her attention to Brian. "Brian has an idea that may help you defeat them. He is a physicist and knows the physics of clouds and lightning."

Maia was skeptical, but she said. "I am all ears. What do you have in mind, Brian?"

"The sword you have in hand is more powerful than you realize." Brian replied.

"It's powerful all right. But how can you shoot down ships I can't see?" Maia shook her head in dismay.

"It's called Geledek. It was once the sword of a fallen angel given by the Creator to guard this world. In your hands it is a sword of vengeance to slay the Xibalbans who turned their backs on the Word." Brian emphasized the power behind the sword.

"I cannot fly into the heavens like an angel, so how can I wield the Geledek against the foe?" Maia asked.

"You may not be able to fly but you can strike from here to the clouds." Brian insisted.

Maia lifted the sword as if to strike.

"Wait. Hear me out. Clouds are capacitors of electricity. You can discharge your weapon into the clouds and destroy the enemy. But first you must charge your sword by thrusting it into the ground." Brian held her back to show her how to discharge the weapon.

"How do I know which cloud to aim at?" Maia was eager to strike if she could only see her enemy but they were hidden.

"We are in communication with the Nishi starship. They have relayed the positions of Xibalban vessels in the clouds." Koko disclosed secret information to her.

"Very well, let's get going. Do you have a position?" Maia was ready and rarin' to go.

"Yes we do. Right above our position are a number of pirate ships ready to strike. They are honing in our infrared signal." Koko told her.

"Should I strike now?" Maia asked for confirmation.

"First thrust the sword into the ground. Then lift and discharge the lightning bolt into the clouds." Brian instructed.

No sooner had Brian spoken the words than Maia thrust the sword into the earth. Then she lifted the Geledek toward the clouds. A blue electric aura glowed around her as she discharged a bolt of lightning into the clouds. Above lightning dazzled through the cloud lighting it up, then there was a burst of red and thunder rolling in the heavens.

Aboard the Xibalban flagship, Drago commander of the fleet, wagged his tail in fear when the hull was breached and the ship was ripped in half. He gave the command to abandon ship. Before any crew could board transports, another explosion burst the vessel asunder and it exploded in a cataclysm. Another cloud burst into fireworks as Maia lifted the Geledek in fury. One by one the Xibalban pirate ships burst in a spectacular scene of light and fireworks. All seven of the Xibalban ships were destroyed. There were no survivors among the Xibalbans. They were utterly defeated at the hands of Maia. The Hutan looked up into the heavens to watch the spectacle. They cried out as the Xiblaban pirates fell to their fiery deaths. They would remember this night the sky burned with fire and the clouds were lit up by lightning wielded by the Queen of the Forest.

Celebrations continued through the night in the Hutan villages. Kurun brought the people together in a central village protected by walls of rock on all sides. Cyrene and her warriors arrived before dawn. They were all very tired from fighting the Xibalbans and in need of care. The Hutans welcomed them and took the weary warriors to hot spring pools on the side of the mountain nearby. When Maia met with Cyrene and a delegation of Neyalan who had come to visit, Cyrene introduced Maia to other Nephali who had come to the aid of the Hutan. Dukun of the Neyalan came to greet Maia and thank her for vanquishing the Xibalban pirates.

"Oh, Queen Maia, we Neyalans wish to extend our gratitude for your courage and fortitude in the face of such great danger. You have saved the day!" Dukun jumped and danced for joy.

"I am pleased to receive you and your people here. Only recently have I come to this place and been greatly received. It is quite overwhelming for me. I wish to bestow this sword to you. I understand you are the rightful owners." Maia graciously surrendered the sword.

"That is true dear Queen. But we fear the danger may not be over and we do not know how to wield it. However we have heard that the Nishi can put it to good use against the Xibalban pirates." Dukun spoke wisely.

"I would like to visit these Nishi you speak of. I have heard good tidings about these people from a faraway planet." Maia spoke her eyes gleaming.

Cyrene smiled and said. "We can take you to the Nishi starship. We could arrange a tour of the ship and you could meet other Nephali like yourself

"Could you take me there soon? I would like to meet the Nephali and warriors who fought against these aggressors, the Naga and the Xibalbans." Maia was eager to meet new friends.

Cyrene replied. "Yes, we would be pleased to take you. We can leave in the morning."

Tim arrived with an assembly of Hutan who had been hiding in the forest. Maia was thrilled to see him especially with the throng of Hutan who followed him. He was so magical showing up on this distant planet just when she needed him most. She felt lost in this place until he came to remind her that someone loved her. He wasn't a warrior or a hero like Will Powers or Cyrene. He had a talent for growing plants and caring for animals. She liked that he was humble and understanding. She still carried his letter he wrote to her before he was lost. Now they were together again.

Brian and Koko were present at the celebration. Both were amazed at the graciousness of Maia and the happiness of the Hutan people. The food and drink were wonderful and the festivities were a glorious show of color and dance. The Hutan were fantastic dancers performing acrobatic feats and jumps over fire and swords. Brian, however, was eager to get back to the ship and see his wife and daughter.

At daybreak Maia left with Cyrene leading a troop of Neyalan through the forest to a transport at the edge of the forest. From there they would embark on the transport across the savannah to the Nishi ship near the citadel. Tim walked alongside her and talked of his travels on Oceanus. She wished that she would have been there with him. Hearing him talk of life in a pristine world free of civilization was exciting to her. Tim had travelled back in time to the Ice Age. Now, she was on another planet in a forest of green. But the ogres of civilization attacked on all sides seeking to destroy the life of the forest. She was willing to give up the Geledek if only she could live in peace. Light was diffused in the forest coming in burst at openings where large trees fell. She could see an opening ahead and the horizon came into view. Soon, they were walking through grass and the sun was beating down.

Cyrene detected a ship above a ridge a mile to the east. She had the eyes of an eagle.

"There is a Naga ship heading our way! Maia prepare to fire if it approaches!" Cyrene warned her.

"I see it now. It is coming very fast upon us!" Maia reacted quickly.

Maia thrust her sword into the earth. The ship fired a blast near the transport and missed. Maia lifted the Geledek and aimed at the ship as it turned away. A bolt of lightning shot forth, and hit the ship in the rear. It careened out of control and crash landed a half mile southeast of their position. Cyrene led the troop into the transport. Koko piloted the transport to the wrecked Naga ship. Koko set the craft down near the Naga ship which was of considerable size over 100 meters in length. The transport was fully armed to fill the larger ship with holes and Koko was standing by to do so. Cyrene, leader of the expedition, gave the command to board the enemy ship.

"Away team, prepare weapons for assault on enemy." Cyrene ordered.

Neyalan warriors were well equipped with blasters that could blast through ship hulls and hatches. They carried laser swords for close combat and they were experienced in ship to ship combat. Koko attempted to communicate with the Nagas, but he received no return. Koko blasted a hole in the side of the ship to rock the occupants. After a few minutes, some of the belligerents began to show themselves and to exit through a door not damaged on the side of the ship.

A strange tall being emerged from the ship among the Nagas. Its skin had the complexion and texture of the Xibalban creatures, yet its physique was more erect and agile. The head of the creature was distinct, different from the brutish appearance of the Xibalban minions. Biru knew this creature as a lord of the Xibalbans, leader of the minions who fought under him. This was the first glimpse of a Xibalban lord for any of these onlookers besides Biru. He was a scary creature with horns on his head, deep set piercing eyes, a long beaked nose, and long limbs on a slender physique. He did not cower like the others but brazenly walked toward the party of warriors with sword in hand. Neyalan warriors singled him out and surrounded him. He bellowed in a loud voice.

"You mortals, I pity you. Why do you fight against what is inevitable? We Xiblabans will swallow your planet and spit you out. Death is coming to you all. I am the Blood Gatherer. Soon your blood will be upon me to quench my anger." Cuchumaquic spoke arrogantly.

"Nephali, thrust your swords into the earth! Warriors, come here behind us. We will stand against this boaster." Cyrene commanded.

"Brave lady, do you wish to cross swords with me?" Cuchumaquic taunted her.

Cyrene remained quiet. Neyalan warriors retreated behind the Nephali for protection. A blue glow emanated from the Nephali in a sphere around the warriors. Maia lifted her sword and spoke to the strange demon.

"Death will come to us as you say, demon. But not today, you have offended the One who created you and all life. Your pride has destroyed any goodness in your soul." Maia spoke in a commanding voice.

Cuchumaquic cut her off in a fury of anger. He waved his sword above his head. Flames emerged from the sword and he grinned with delight.

"You dare to oppose the lord of death? You know nothing of the black hole sun and its power! Now you will meet your fate!" Cuchumaquic boomed in a loud vulgar voice.

Cuchumaquic swung his sword of flaming fire at the Nephali. It cut a swath of trees behind them and left the grass burning in a great fire, but the Nephali and the warriors were untouched. Cuchumaquic was stunned.

Maia aimed her sword at Cuchumaquic and shot a burst of lightning into his belly. Instantly, he dropped his sword, his flesh melted away, leaving his skeleton behind. There was no more lord of death on the savannah. Biru and the Nagas dropped to their knees in homage to the Nephali.

Cyrene led the party to the transport. Maia was weary of wielding the Geledek. She longed for a simpler, peaceful life.

As Tim walked beside her, she offered him her hand. Together they walked toward the transport that would take them to the Nishi starship. Maia hoped to go to Tengoku, home of the Nishi. Koko fired up the transport, and off they went.

Powers, in a Nishi jet, had witnessed the Naga vessel crash. His patrol was over and he swung his craft toward the starship to land.

On board the starship, Powers hurried to sickbay to see Helen. On entering sickbay, he asked the nurses to see his friend. Galatea recognized Will and allowed him to see Helen. He entered her room. Her eyes were closed. Quietly, he went to her side. She looked pale but she was breathing. He knelt down beside her and whispered her name. He looked at her face hoping she would wake. He touched her hand, holding it in his. He thought she needed rest. He kissed her gently on the cheek. She stirred, a glow filled her cheeks and she opened her eyes.

"Will." She looked into his eyes.

"Helen." He smiled, at her.

"Oh Will, you came back to me." Helen spoke faintly.

"I am here to stay." Will spoke gently to her.

She reached out to hold him, and he took her in his arms.

"Are you feeling better?" Will sensed she was ethereal, he was afraid she might slip away.

"I still feel weak. The nurse said I am recovering. I do feel better but too weak to walk." Helen spoke in a low voice.

"I was afraid you might not make it. That was a deadly shot you took to the leg." Will was truly concerned with her health.

"I was unconscious for days. I did not feel the pain until I woke a few days ago. But the wound has healed somehow." Helen was encouraged to hear his voice.

"It is a wonder what the Nishi can do in healing people." Will hoped for the best.

"Galatea assured me that with exercise, I could walk again." Helen replied.

"That is encouraging. Did she mention what kind of exercise you would be doing?"

"She mentioned swimming and physical therapy, like massages." Helen said.

"I suppose you will have to rest awhile longer before you go swimming." Will did not want to tire her with too much talk.

"Yes, but I am getting tired of lying in bed." Helen was eager to walk with Will.

"I hope you don't blame this on me. You wouldn't be here if you had not met me." Will blamed himself.

"Oh I remember the night I met you Will. It was I that wanted to go on an adventure. You were the man I was looking for. I am glad I met you. I just didn't expect to meet fire breathing Dragons, ruthless Nagas and horrible Xibalbans." Helen was overjoyed to have her man at her side.

"You are a brave lady, Helen. I want to stay by your side if you will have me." Will wanted to marry her.

"You came back to me. I want to be your mate in life, Will." Helen kissed Will but she still felt weak. She sighed as if in pain.

Will held her and felt her pulse, it was strong. He hoped she would live. Suddenly she winced and trembled.

Will was alarmed. "Are you in pain? Should I call the nurse?"

"No, I am just tired from the medicine. I will rest now." Helen closed her eyes momentarily.

"All right, I will come and see you tomorrow. Goodnight." Will kissed her on the cheek.

"Goodnight, Will." Helen spoke gently and closed her eyes.

As Will was walking out, he saw Galatea.

"Galatea, may I speak with you?" Will was despondent.

"Of course, Will." Galatea responded and listened.

"Helen is weak. Will she recover?" Will hoped for some good news.

"I cannot say for sure. We are all praying for her." Galatea gave him an honest appraisal and hoped for a miracle.

"I don't want to lose her." Will sighed.

"Pray for her. Come and visit in the afternoon tomorrow." Galatea entreated.

"Thank you, I will do so. Goodnight." Will assented with a nod.

"Goodnight Will. We will look after Helen." Galatea consoled him.

Will was troubled, he strolled toward the Arboretum. He could hear the falling water on the rocks and birds singing. He sat on a bench beside a pool and prayed for his lady's recovery.

Tatiana marveled at the spaciousness of the ship. She went to the gymnasium and worked out in a room that seemed like a trail in the forest. The longer she walked it seemed to go on and on. There were also hills and mountains in the distance and the sun was setting over the horizon. She thought it must be an illusion yet there was earth beneath her feet.

After her walk she went to a swimming pool that led to an underground grotto. She swam underwater to the grotto and met other people bathing in the hot water. Feeling refreshed she took a walk and looked for shops. She had taken some gold jewelry from Biru's treasure hoping to cash in later. She was hoping to find a nice dress and shoes to wear, but she could find no shops for fancy clothes, cosmetics, pocket books or anything of the kind.

She was upset, wondering what kind of people these Nishi were. They all wore simple clothes, yet they had this exquisite ship. Then again she thought the pirates had plenty of things she wanted but treated her like a slave. She wondered if she put herself into the lair of pirates because of her materialism.

She thought about her friend Valentin. His values of putting luxuries over people brought him to ruin. She remembered how she treated Will putting him down for his simple ways, calling him stupid. Walking along she found the Arboretum, there was Will sitting on a bench with his head in his hands.

Concerned, Tatiana said. "Will, are you All right? Is there something wrong?"

He looked up. "I was praying for a friend." Will replied grief stricken.

"I'm sorry I interrupted you." Tatiana replied politely.

Will kept thinking of Helen.

Tatiana was curious. "Was your friend hurt?"

"Yes, she is in the infirmary." Will replied weakly.

"Is she going to be all right?" Tatiana tried to be sympathetic.

"She was seriously wounded. The nurses are not sure of the outcome." Will was shaken.

"How did this happen to her?" Tatiana thought of those nasty Nagas.

"We were in a squad fighting Xibalbans invading the Naga citadel. A Xibalban was about to bite my leg when she shot him. Then another shot her in the leg."

"She is a brave lady. I suppose she is your lady now." Tatiana replied.

"Yes. She has been since you left me." Will admitted.

"I'm sorry Will. I wish you and your friend the best." Tatiana sighed and left Will to himself. She wanted to say she had made a mistake that she would regret for the rest of her life, but she didn't want to meddle. Will was hurting, and for once, she would be compassionate.

She left Will and continued her walk through the arboretum. She sighed hurting inside knowing she lost Will and would not be intimate with him again. She could not enjoy the beauty of the water falling down from the canopy in the diffused light and the song of birds. She had hoped so much to apologize to Will and come back to him. But it was too late. She felt like a prisoner, lost far from the home she knew.

What would she do now? she asked herself. Maybe she could find someone who could tell her about her lost home Oceanus. A realization arose in her that her planet was like a jewel in the universe, unique and beautiful. Like the love she had lost, she must treasure it and hope to return someday. So much she had taken for granted she now wanted to find a way to bring it back. There were many things she remembered that she owned and cherished but now she thought of how the beauty of her world now vanished from her sight. If she returned what would her town look like after so much destruction?

As Tatiana walked through the arboretum, a group of people came into view. A lady attired in a feathery dress caught her attention. Her eyes were bright aquamarine, shining over golden brown skin of her face and arms. Raven black hair flowed down her back. She walked with grace among her company of admirers. Tatiana was envious of her stunning beauty and the attention she received. Even birds alighted on her shoulders. Tatiana heard one of the lady's retinue mention her name.

"Oh, Maia, our dear queen of the forest, will you give your mighty sword to the Nishi and forsake us Hutans?" Kurun had heard Maia would be departing from Pataloka.

"My dear friend Kurun, I cannot defend your people from the merciless Xibalbans. You need the help of the

Nishi to protect your world from their depredations."
Maia declared.

"As an elder of the Hutans, I trust your judgement. I
only fear you may leave us." Kurun acquiesced.

"If I do leave you, it will only be for a short time.
Cyrene will stay to look after you." Maia encouraged
him.

"Why would you leave us? You are our Queen!" Kurun
still felt abandoned.

"The Nishi have invited me to Tengoku. I may be
transformed on Tengoku. Only then will I will be able
to be your true queen." Maia underlined the necessity
of her journey.

"I have heard of this Tengoku. It is a world full of
wonders and heavenly delights. The people and wild
creatures live together in harmony." Kurun extolled
the ocean planet.

"So too have I heard wise Kurun. Would you
recommend I visit this shrine of nature?" Maia adroitly
asked for his advice.

"I do indeed but we will miss you." Kurun replied
graciously.

"Cyrene is a more capable leader than I. She is a full-
fledged Nephali!" Maia downplayed her role as Queen.

"Yes, I have seen her in battle. No Naga can stand
against her" Kurun conceded.

Tatiana wondered what this talk was all about. It
seemed like a fairy tale. Yet here she was on a
starship lightyears away from Oceanus. Maybe such a
place did exist. She wanted to go there too. Maybe she
could buy a ticket but she didn't have any money.

Another Nishi Starship came into orbit around
Pataloka, home planet of the Naga race. News traveled

swiftly from the new visitors of recent developments on Oceanus. Belinda had heard the news broadcast in a dining room that was open to communication from the outside. She was walking with friends toward the arboretum when she noticed Tatiana just leaving.

"Tatiana, what a surprise it is to see you here!" Belinda gazed at her with eyes wide open.

"Wow! It is for me as well. How did you come to be here?" Tatiana replied with a cheerful voice.

"Tatiana, these are my friends Rory and Brian. We have come on this ship on a mission to rescue Maia." Belinda put out her hands toward her friends.

"Oh, I am so glad to meet you. I see your mission was a success. I saw Maia talking in the arboretum." Tatiana was excited to meet people from Oceanus.

"How are you Tatiana? I heard you were captured by the Nagas." Rory winked at her.

"Yes. Will Powers rescued me. I really don't deserve it" Tatiana felt remorse.

"Oh, come now, Tatiana. We all make mistakes in life. Be glad you are here and safe." Brian commiserated with her.

"Oh I am glad but I feel so out of place." Tatiana thought of a song "I wish I had a river I could skate away on". Now she wished for a river instead of tears.

"You have been in a terrible ordeal. When you are feeling up to it, go to the entertainment hall and relax. Have some fun!" Belinda encouraged her.

"There is an entertainment hall here?" Tatiana loved to dance.

"Yes, the Nishi really know how to keep your spirits up." Belinda prodded her.

"Please tell me where I can find this enchanting place." Tatiana pleaded.

"Just go straight down this hall and you will hear the music playing." Rory replied grinning.

"Thanks. Are you going there too?" Tatiana was hoping for company.

"Not just yet. We have a meeting to see Maia, but we may catch up to you later." Belinda suggested.

"Hope to see you then." Tatiana waved goodbye.

Belinda smiled. "Have a good time."

Belinda and her friends walked into the tranquil arboretum and soon they were immersed in the sounds of chirping birds in a tropical rainforest. Maia was speaking to a Celaeno, Glaucus and Nereus. The three Nephali were discussing Maia's proposed trip to Tengoku.

"Belinda, how do you fare? Do you have tidings of Oceanus?" Nereus beckoned her.

"Yes, I have just heard news of Oceanus." Belinda reported.

"Well, out with it, girl. What have you heard?" Glaucus was anxious.

"Admiral Tolpiltzin has been captured. The Nagas have been defeated!" Belinda exclaimed with exhilaration.

"How was the devil captured? He is such a slippery serpent!" Celaeno remarked.

"His own troops, the K'ny, rebelled against him. They are holding him for ransom, but none of the Nagas will pay to free him." Belinda disclosed.

"Why would the K'ny rise up against their leader?" Nereus marveled at the news.

'Many of the K'ny recognized their kith and kin among the people of Oceanus. Many adopted the religion of their kin on Oceanus. They abandoned their posts and left the army." Rory said.

"That must have come as a big surprise to the Naga commanders." Nereus understood the consequences of widespread mutiny.

"The news is that the K'ny troops mutinied first in the Near East and then the movement gained momentum across the globe." Rory continued his story.

"The K'ny were known as disciplined troops trained as soldiers from youth. How could this happen?" Celaeno thought of the K'ny as clones of the Nagas.

'It is a mystery. But it happened spontaneously starting in the Ukraine. Naga commanders were cut down by their own troops." Brian stated what he had seen and heard via live broadcast on the bridge of the Calypso.

"What will happen to these K'ny now that they are stranded on Oceanus?" Celaeno reckoned the K'ny would be singled out for revenge.

"I guess we will have to wait and see." Belinda remarked.

"This is wonderful news! Peace will now come to Oceanus." Maia was optimistic.

"Yes we all hope so. Grace be upon you, dear Queen." Brian payed her homage.

"I have played a small part in this struggle. Any one of these brave Nephali could well have done as well or better. Fear was in my heart when I fled into the forest." Maia felt uneasy about being treaty as Ronalty.

"We know you as our Queen because you overcame your fear and confronted a terrible bloodthirsty foe." Rory bowed before her.

"We know you as our Queen ever since you adopted the Hutan and sheltered them under your wings." Belinda curtsied to her.

"Come closer, my friends." Maia opened her arms to embrace her admirers. The trio of Nephali embraced those who embraced in a circle of love and friendship.

Koko came into the arboretum with two Nishi by his sides. It looked to Maia that he was on urgent business. He approached Maia to speak.

"Have you heard the news? Federation ships from all across the galaxy have arrived to conference with Admiral Mitsuo."

"What could this portend to us on this lonely planet?" Belinda remarked.

"I believe the Xibalbans are massing to attack another star system with the remainder of their fleet." Koko surmised.

"Is there never any peace in this galaxy?" Rory replied with displeasure.

"Not until the Xibalbans are utterly defeated." Koko announced.

"Does this mean we are going into battle again and chasing these miserable Xibalbans?" Maia groped over the futility of war.

"You may go to Tengoku." Koko suggested.

Timothy showed up behind Koko, who was walking through the arboretum.

"Timothy, will you go to Tengoku with me?" Maia asked.

"I will." Forthright he replied and hugged her.

Brian could only think of the control room of Galatea and how it traveled through the vastness of space. Actually it did not move like a rocket to the moon. Galatea was a quantum disc that accelerated subatomic particles. Nishi technicians controlled the frequency of the magnetron to resonate with the magnetic field as it travelled in a vector of spacetime. Throughout the fabric of the fullerene shell were sensors that instantaneously sent signals of electromagnetic energy from the nearby stars in the course of the spacecraft's trajectory.

Brian learned how the Nishi manipulated the disc to align with these forces so the craft would travel without encountering any mass. In this way the spacecraft followed a spiral path through galaxies to its destination at perceived velocities far exceeding the speed of light within the Heliosphere, for the speed of light was constant throughout the universe. Whenever light shined on matter, photons were released from the outer shell at the constant speed of light as measure by the scientists of Oceanus. However magnetic fields of stars carried the light signal across the cosmos just as photons were held by the nucleus of atoms of the microcosm.

"Brian make ready. Headquarters is calling for you to come to the control room." Commanded Koko.

Brian shook out of the revelry, looking around the room to see that people were moving around him. In a moment he had seen the spacecraft as it was moved in a spiral through the cosmos. Galatea was a living creature like a whale finding its way in a vast ocean. A whale would use its melon to echolocate through space. Galatea used its fullerene skin to locate magnetic fields to navigate. It was time for him to join the crew.

"Aye, Aye sir, I'm on my way." Brian obeyed and set forth.

Koko escorted Maia and the Nephali to her room to make preparations for her journey. There was no time to waste. The *Calypso* would be leaving in a few hours to Tengoku for the chosen ones. All noncombatants disembarked from the Calypso and went on board another vessel to a planet in the Pleiades star system. It was an ocean planet like Oceanus prepared by the Nishi to accept refugees from the war. Tatiana was one of many refugees departing to this new world far from home. She was anxious about the journey. Everyone going had watched a video about the wonders of this place among the stars. It was a much larger planet about the size of Jupiter. There was no strife among the inhabitants other than natural prey and predator struggles among the animals.

In the morning, Will Powers awoke and went to the hospital to see Helen. He hoped she was feeling better but worried that she might not be able to overcome her grievous injury. The nurse allowed him to visit her telling him she was now awake. He pulled the curtain aside as he entered her room. Helen was standing by the window looking out. She turned around to face Will.

Will looked at her and said. "Helen, you are feeling well?"

"I feel fine." Helen smiled.

Will held her in his arms, so grateful she had recovered.

They looked out the window to see the Nishi fleet departing.

The *Calypso* and allies departed to confront the Xibalbans in one final battle.

NAGA HISTORY

Long ago in a galaxy faraway dwelled a people living on a lonely planet. They were fortunate to have a bright sun and a tropical climate, The Nagas flourished for millions of years on the fruitful planet revolving around their sun RA. The planet was covered with tropical rainforests intertwined with savannahs from the equator to temperate midlatitides. The poles were ocean free of ice. The seas were shallow but the land was full of contrasts with tall mountains, deep valleys, plateaus, lowlands by the sea and plenty of volcanic activity.

Like the people of Oceanus, the Nagas were descended from primates. However, only a few mammal species survived because of the rise of voracious predatory dinosaurs. Mammals originated in the far northern region which was very cold and not suitable for the dinosaurs who preferred the warm climate of the tropics. As the continents drifted, the poles shifted into the seas and the lands of the mammals drifted south.

In the beginning, the ancestors of the Naga contended with terrible carnivore dinosaurs on land and Dragons attacking from above. Being clever, they ate the eggs of their enemies, thereby defeating them at birth and selecting docile ones for training. In this way the Nagas developed allies in their quest for survival, much like the Oceanids adopted wolves and horses.

Naga people were quite dazzling in appearance with iridescent feathers covering their skin. Most of their species had oblong heads with sloping foreheads and bulging cerebellums, large ears, prominent beak-like noses, and large mouths full of sharp teeth, though there was much diversity among races in stature, size, strength, colors, agility, intelligence and culture. One common trait among all races was six digits on both their feet and hands. The fingers being long and bony, and six toes spread widely over a cushioned foot. Nagas hunted for small animals, like reptiles, amphibians, insects, birds and their eggs. Most of their world was covered in rainforests and food was plentiful. Nagas preferred hunting on the edge of the forests in grasslands where prey was more exposed.

At first, the Nagas lived in large communal nests high up in trees. As they ventured into the grasslands, canyon, meadows and streams below the mountains, the Nagas embraced a scavenging lifestyle always on the lookout for large predators. The mighty Allosaurs reigned supreme over land from mountains, to the sea. Any Naga found out in the open would be prey to the undisputed tyrant of Tlalocan. The rainforest may have beeen a paradise but outside its walls of trees lay a dangerous open arena of blood and gore.

Foraging in the savannah favored Individuals who were more upright as well as having dexterous fingers and feet for running. Small terapods that were captured alive were not always eaten but trained as pets. Nagas kept these pets like dogs and used them to help find, kill prey and warn of large predators nearby. Within a few generations of leaving the forest, communities of Nagas were expanding at the edge of the forest, the fear of Allosaurs still imprinted on their brain. Allosaurs would raid at night sending the colonies of Nagas and their pets back up into the trees for safety. There was no winning the war against these monsters with only small doglike terapods to fight with. Another ally was discovered by the Nagas in their forays in the savannah, fire.

It was discovered that the mighty Allosaurs were terrified of fire started by lightning. Nagas carried this sacred fire on torches to their nest sites beside the forest edge. A single torch was not enough of a deterrent for a charging Allosaur, but a fire surrounding an Allosaur's nest was a disaster that could not be stopped. With fire as an ally, Nagas ventured forth into the savannah with torches to look for eggs and set fires to terrorize the monsters. During this war against the monsters, immense areas of forests were burned, and the enraged Allosaurs exacted revenge upon the colonies of Nagas in the forest. So, began the Jaman Api (Age of Fire), the first period of time when Nagas came into their own, and looked far ahead onto the horizon, but they still had fond memories of the rainforest.

The Naga exodus from the forest came with the domestication of flying reptiles. These pterosaurs had wingspans exceeding ten meters and were capable of carrying the light boned Nagas for extended flights of kilometers. But there were races of Nagas who were built too heavy for the Dragons to carry so these remained in their forest mansions.

So, began the Jaman Penerbangan (Age of Flight). Flying over the grasslands on their trained pterosaurs, opened horizons, territories and expanded the imagination of the Nagas. The joining of Nagas and Pterosaurs created an evolutionary leap for both creatures within the ecosystem. For a Naga and his Dragon were one in appearance and were much more powerful together than as separate creatures. A large pterosaur with a ten-meter wingspan could glide over the savannah for hours looking for dead prey to scavenge or live prey if it were safe to land. Even though these pterosaurs were large they were relatively slow on land and slow to take off in flight. With a Naga equipped with spears and accompanied by a fleet of

Dragons with Naga crew, the combination was nearly invincible, except for the very large theropods like Allosaurs.

The main target of the Naga Dragon pair was large dinosaur eggs, much of the booty was eaten on, but a few were carried back to the Naga nest site at the edge of the forest. Nagas protected their Dragons from small, predacious terapods, but with the sudden coming of an Allosaur, the entire colony would evacuate and take to the air to escape certain death. Over the course of thousands of years, a war lasted between Allosaurs, and the Naga Dragons. Initially, the Allosaurs found the colonies and devastated the colonies nearly decimating the populations of both Naga and Dragons. Face to face, the PasangaNaga (Naga Dragon pairs) were no match for Allosaurs. Nagas kept up the fight to the end, capturing young pterosaurs for training, and training young Nagas to pair with a Dragon and then to go out to battle the Allosaurs. Allosaurs had a weakness in their defense. They were not social creatures. Though the Allosaur mother looked after her eggs and young, the father soon left after copulation, leaving the mother to raise the young alone. Nagas exploited this weakness setting up ruses for the Allosaur mothers. An Allosaur mother would have to leave the nest to find food, and while she was away the Nagas attacked from the air, breaking and eating the eggs.

Yet the PasangaNaga failed to defeat the Allosaurs. There were other dangerous foes, like velociraptors, that attacked them and large oviraptors that competed with the Nagas for eggs. Only a bringing together of all the Nagas would insure victory.

A Kepala (chief) named Anu united all the puaks (Naga clans) under his leadership to clear the way through the open savannah and defeat Allosaur.

Anu brought together the HutaNaga (thick limbed Nagas of the forests) with their dromaeosaur dogs and the RingaNaga (light limbed Nagas) mounted on pterosaurs. Anu and the leaders of the flocks made a plan for the forest flocks to be the infantry carrying torches. The infantry on the ground would follow the Nagas, soaring above and doing reconnaissance. Together, they attacked the Allosaur nests by ambush and retreat and defended each other with fire and spear. The battle between the huge terapods and the Nagas and their allies continued for thousands of years as raiding parties of Nagas destroyed the eggs of their foes rather than taking them on face to face. In the end the Nagas wiped out the population of Allosaurs and their cousins by going after the young.

With the defeat of their ancient adversaries, the Nagas had a dominant hold over the land from forest to sea. There remained many dangerous dinosaurs freely roaming some in packs, but the huge tyrants were gone. Nagas who had left the forests found shelters in caves and then villages behind stockades built by sturdy heavy limbed ones. In their exploration of this new territory, light Nagas discovered gems that glittered in the sunlight. These jewels they carried back to the villages for their tribe's amazement and veneration.

A number of colonies spread out as population grew in the open savannah rivalling the forest edge community. Peaceful trade existed between the diverse tribes of Nagas and a currency of teeth from Allosaur remains developed. Finding jewels upended the trade in teeth and sent a flurry of excitement through the tribes. Expeditions were funded by companies of traders to find more jewels.

So, began the Jaman Permata (Age of Jewels). It was a time of expansion into the rocky slopes of the mountains in search of precious gems and a growing religious cult centered on the light emanating from the crystals.

The funding of expeditions by rich Nagas sent traders across lands far away from their small communities. Communication about new ideas and materials spread like wildfire across the savannah. Enterprising individuals found ores of metals. Soon these ores were put to the test in the fire of hearths and metals were discovered and shaped into objects of veneration. Later spear points and knives were made to extend the use of their arms. Others found ways to project metal points without the use of spears, ergo Jaman Logam (the Age of Metal) began.

Conflicts arose over trade and were often settled with the use of these new weapons tipped with copper points and swords. Renegade traders far from their home village banded together, raided villages, and then stole away to secret hideouts. Villages combined to form confederacies to protect the tribes from marauding bandits. Priests of the villages sought help from divining the light from the stars and crystals. Renegades found ores that made stronger tools and weapons so the conflict escalated with the takeover of villages.

During this time visitors from a nearby star system made contact with the Nagas. They called themselves the Nishi and spoke in a strange tongue incomprehensible to the Nagas. The Nagas spoke in a code of clicks, chirps, and buzzing sounds. In contrast, the Nishi language was of discrete words and phrases. The Nishi endeavored to overcome this obstacle with a translating device.

Nishi anthropologists had studied the Nagas secretly for centuries and developed a vocabulary of Naga code that could be transliterated for trade and basic communication. It was a device that could be worn around the wrist or arm. Once activated it would translate for the wearer Naga to Nishi or vice versa. Among the Naga were an intelligent caste of people who were capable of imagination and rational thought. In the tumult of recent revolution they had arisen to leadership among many of the clans. Together with the priests they convinced the rabble to tolerate these strangers. The Nishi attempted to teach a few of these Naga a select spoken language of the Oceanids, a feat they thought would be feasible. A trade developed between the Nagas and Nishi who needed jewels for space exploration. In turn, the Nagas asked for technical help in developing agricultural practices, mining, transport, medicine, and metallurgy.

Tlalocan's rainforests were diminished because of fires spread in the expansion of the savannah. The planet had few mammals and food resources were low due to overconsumption, so the Nishi provided a variety of rodent species that would quickly populate and supply food needs. The Nishi warned Nagas to confine the rodents to areas suitable for crops and not allow the rodents to enter the rainforest. Small contingents of Nishi were allowed to live on the planet to teach the Nagas how to manage the rodents and the growing of crops for them.

Trade between the Nishi and the Nagas flourished for millennia. An aristocracy ruled over the tribes to hold renegades in check. Among the aristocracy, a genetic divide began to develop after thousands of years of isolation from the forest tribes. Those Nagas who lived in the savannah lost much of their feathery coating on the skin. A colorful feathery crest remained on top of their cranium and sometimes down their spine. With the loss of feathers over most of the body, the skin became naked with a silky feel and a variety of color, usually bluish. Among the nelayan fisher folk, they also lost much of their feathery coating like the savannah folk but their skin had a slight scaly feel.

Roads were built and schools of technology were erected to teach arts and sciences, what the Nagas thought as sakti (magic). A colony of Nishi remained on the planet, but the Nagas had no interest in traveling to the Nishi planet. They were somewhat xenophobic despite their long alliance. There were few among the Naga who ventured into the realm of science. The horde of Naga was obsessed with astrology and magic, divination, and gambling.

At the end of the Jaman Sakti, the Age of Magic, the leadership of the Nagas faltered. Rodents had invaded the rainforest and were out of control. Food resources were dwindling and the decimation of the rainforests quickly turned these areas into deserts. The ruling caste fought among themselves over trade, territory and power. Battles expanded into wars, and great expanses of land were laid waste.

It was at this time that trade with the Nishi was cutoff. Nagas were suspicious of the Nishi and blamed them for their problems. Many of the Nishi colonists left Tlalocan. A few of the Nishi were allowed to stay and continue teaching Nagas in the technical schools. Some Nishi attempted to teach Nagas the Law of Peace and Tranquility but these were banished to a deserted region on the planet. They were thence known as Riskani and were not allowed to teach. Naga aristocracy forbade persecution of the Riskani because they yearned to know the secrets of the cosmos.

Nagas ventured onto the seas to search for food. Up to this time very little was known of the seas and the life within besides coastal fishing. It was the Nishi belief that they should let the Nagas learn on their own with a minimum of help. Naga villagers had heard stories from Nelayan (fisher folk) trading at markets of sea serpents attacking crews of Nelayan and swallowing them whole. Hearing these stories firsthand from kin folk in their villages incensed the Nagas. Agung an elder nelayan told a story to keluarga (kin folk) about a legendary beast of the sea.

"Before there was the forest there was sea, and before there was the mighty Allosaur there was in the deep a sea dragon of terrifying power. Before the sea was surga (sky), and then came geledek (lightning) out of the heavens. It struck the lautan (ocean), and TopaNaga (Typhoon sea Dragon) was born. From her all life, sprang into the sea and crawled onto the land. She rules the sea and devours all who opposes her. Beware of fishing in her waters without praying to her spirit. It was from her we sprang and pay homage we must to her in the days of old now forgotten. In her eyes burns a fire that freezes the heart of the boldest Naga."

Nevertheless, Nelayans organized a party to build a larger ship to take on the sea serpents. A few months later, the day came to launch an eighty-foot long boat from a harbor on the coast of the northern sea. It boasted a high prow to take on the high seas and winds. Forty swarthy Nelayans boarded the vessel equipped with weapons to capture the sea serpent.

After a few hours of rowing, a monstrous hump was spotted beside the boat. Suddenly the boat tipped to one side. The Nagas quickly shifted to the other side. Kana stared at the sea beast. It was half as long as the boat, then its huge head appeared with a row of daggers in its mouth. The neck was half as long as its body. They grabbed spears and grappling hooks. Then it came at them, slashing, knocking them into the water, and thrashing its long powerful neck at them, their spears falling out of their hands as they fell in the sea.

Kana was still in the boat with a few other Nagas. They watched helplessly the sea beast held a Naga in its gaping mouth, crushing him with its teeth, and then tossing him a distance into the sea. Then it grabbed another Naga out of the sea and tossed him then before it slid under a wave and grabbed the Naga and dove down. Kana and the other nine survivors still on the boat got hold of oars and made a quick getaway back to the shore. When news reached of this disaster and loss of so many Nagas, the people were shocked and dismayed. It was decided not to risk any more adventures in the northern sea.

The Kepala, (leaders of the Naga), decided to open the Sekolah (schools of learning) and seek the knowledge of the Riskani who lived in the mountains of the northern lands, a region too cold for the Naga. A few Riskani agreed to return and teach willing Naga. When asked about the sea serpents, the Riskani feigned no knowledge of these strange creatures. However, they were willing to teach the physical sciences to aspiring candidates.

In the years that followed, advances were made in technology of structural engineering and rocket propulsion. The Nagas were obsessed with the stars and desired to travel into space, though they had never invented the wheel or made any kind of vehicle as such. There were no aero planes or helicopters designed, yet rockets were their passion. Naga youths' favorite toy were rockets which they made out of homemade stuff. Among the Nagas were a few who excelled in binary math as they envisioned their world in code. Many of the Naga could not vocalize in a fluent language but uttered in clicks and chirps to communicate. Only a few learned to speak in analog tongue. Among the elite, the study of an Oceanid tongue was considered a prerequisite for attending Sekolah. The Riskani were puzzled by the Nagas' fascination with the stars as they observed that the Nagas were not interested in exploring the seas on their own planet.

A large colorful moon rotated about Tlalocan, and the planet had a very long day and night compared to Oceanus. Nagas worshipped the moon and connected rain and the fertility of the soil with the full moon. They called the moon Lera Wulan, an old male who mated with the earth, Tana Ekan, a young female. Jaman Bintang (Age of Stars) began with the exploration of outer space. Their first journey was to visit the moon. Many of the Nagas were against this incursion onto the home of Lera Wulan. The Kepala, the leading class, overruled objections of the forest clans and village clans, stating that Lera Wulan invited them for a short visit. There was much excitement about the moon trip, but it was not a place where the Nagas could live. No atmosphere and no life was found on the moon, so the Nagas would have to look elsewhere to find a new colony.

Shortly after the Nagas successful visit to their moon, they were visited by an alien race from a distant star. From the viewpoint of Oceanus, this star was 11,000 Light Years distant in the constellation of Scorpius. They called their lost world Xibalba, a planet that had been swallowed when their sun went supernova and a black hole ate the entire solar system. This race of reptilian humanoids was bitter about their fate and the loss of their planet. They drifted through galaxies plundering the planets they found habitable. These ruthless intergalactic pirates came to the paradise of Tlalocan with its verdant rainforests and lush savannahs at a time when the

Nagas yearned for knowledge and wondered about life outside of their world.

The Lords of Xibalba needed jewels to pilot their spacecraft. In exchange for jewels, the Xibalbans taught the Nagas space technology so they could gather jewels for them. These creatures were upright and tall, large heads with horns on their foreheads, large eyes and nostrils. They were fearsome creatures but clever in dealing with aliens for trade. For a time the Xibalbans ruled over the Nagas. The Lord of Xilbalba wielded a weapon that resembled a staff that could produce lightning. In the generations that followed Nagas worshipped these creatures that wielded Geledek (lightning) and were enslaved until the downfall of the gods.

It was no wonder Nagas were fascinated with the stars. The people of Oceanus had one brilliant star to gaze upon and banish all other stars until their planet spun around for night time to arrive. On Tlalocan, Nagas were bathed in the warmth of RA, which nurtured life and two other stars were visible as companions during the day. Two moons revolved around Tlalocan causing turbulent tidal currents in the seas. Perhaps, it was for this reason that the Nagas were hesitant to explore the sea and its voracious monsters. They chose to go into space and explore the moons and make bases there. On Tlalocan, cities grew near the sea and rivers which crossed the open lands and the forests where the primeval Hutan lived. The great Allosaurs were long gone and in their place were monsters that conquered the sky. Cathedrals of metal marked the landscape like the pyramids of Egypt, yet inside were a myriad of workers building ships that would be launched across the galaxy. Nagas did not bother with wheels for transportation. They used jet propelled vehicles to go fast across the open lands. Rails were used to transport freight in raw materials to factories. The Ronal Kepala preferred to travel by flying their pet Dragons. Common folk lived near factories and farms and walked to where they had to go unless they were rich enough to have a jet shuttle. Neyalan fisherfolk lived by the sea in villages catching fish to sell to factory workers.

In days of yore, Guntur built a fleet of ships to explore the sea but after his death they rotted on the shore. There was no more exploration of the great sea. It was a mystery and a sacred place of the Dragon that gave birth to all life. After the exodus of the Nishi from Tlalocan only a few of their descendants the Riskani remained living in caves near the sea and forest lands. They were banished after the coming of the Xibalbans but were sought after to pilot the spaceships to the stars.

It was thought by the ascendant Royalty that the Riskani knew of a cosmic code that ruled the stars. It was this cosmic code that was needed to chart the heavens and find another planet that was habitable. Riskani were useful as teachers but were not trusted in political circles, so they kept to themselves, waiting for a time of deliverance.

Some 12,000 years before present (Oceanus time) the Nagas succeeded in finding a habitable planet known as Oceanus, the ocean planet. It was a short journey of six months across 22 light years from Tlalocan. With the help of Xibalban technology, the Nagas built a rocket propelled vehicle capable of attaining light speed and harnessing the galactic magnetic field. However, the Nagas did not fully understand the physics of this feat. After a short visit to Oceanus, the crew of the Naga starship kidnapped a score of young boys and girls under the guise of taking them to the House of the Gods. These captives were brought to Tlalocan and were trained as mercenaries and emissaries of the Naga Empire. These were called the K'ny as they were known on Oceanus as horse riders and raiders.

Those who excelled gained admission to Sekolah, lived in the city and did no work but training. Those who failed were put to work in mines, construction work and serving the elite. After a few centuries, the colony of K'ny grew to thousands, ready to wage war and colonize new territory for their masters. K'ny were taught to honor Raja Hutan, Anu ancestor of the Naga and his consort TopaNaga, Typhoon, sea Dragon. The K'ny elite were trained in the art of warfare, weaponry, strategy, transport, athletic contests, science, technology and linguistics. They came to rival the Naga in physical stamina and intelligence stirring fear and suspicion in the hearts of the ruling kepala.

At this time, a Supernova occurred in a nearby galaxy, and the cosmic ray blast devastated the species of large reptilians on Tlalocan including the Xibalbans who ruled over them. In their weakened state, the Xibalbans were overthrown and killed. The Nagas took the weapons of Geledek and stored them as sacred objects. Worship of Lera Wulan and Tana Ekan was restored to the Nagas, but the Naga ruling class now ruled like Xibalbans. Many of the outlying Naga population had been weakened but recovered within a few generations. The elite Nagas who lived under protective domes were spared from its ill effects, and the K'ny who also lived under domes were spared from the effects of DNA degeneration. The reptilian Xibalbans had preferred to live in an oasis in the desert so they experienced the full effect of the cosmic radiation. The Riskani lived in caves and escaped the ill effects of the radiation. Among the K'ny and Riskani were a few who evidently benefited from the cosmic event as though a code was hidden in the blast. The surviving Nagas who lived in the forest and by the sea were abandoned by the elite, but a few underwent a change in their consciousness. The Kepala retained control due to the devotion of the K'ny. The Naga elite had succumbed to the Xibalban deception of power over nature and its creatures. They had made a contract with the Lords of Death.

Invasion forces of thousands of K'ny were assembled to depart from Tlalocan destination Oceanus, 7000 years before present. Troops were divided into squadrons of Dragon ships from the main fleet of starships. Their target was the fertile region of the Indus Valley, the rising Hindu civilization, the Fertile Crescent and the civilizations of Egypt and Sumer. Emissaries of the Naga and K'ny mercenaries embarked on this intergalactic mission to subdue the people of Oceanus. It was the plan of the Kepala to first contact leaders of Oceanus and bring them under the power of Anu. The worship of the gods of the Nagas was paramount. The people of Oceanus must be persuaded to worship the gods of the Nagas.

First, the Naga dazzled the simple villagers with feats of power and magic. Second, the Naga instructed the people to build temples in honor of the gods. Third, the Naga would demanded sacrifices to the gods.

Fourth, the Naga instructed the people to make idols of the gods to perform rituals and rites to honor the gods.

Initially, the strategy of divide and conquer, creating a special priestly class and the replacement of village communities with city temple plazas was a success. As a result, a large population of humans was trained to mine for precious metal ores and jewels that the Naga needed for their exploration and continued colonization.

Revolution came like a sledgehammer blow to Nagas' plans and legions. In a tremendous battle in India, a hero named of Krishna came out of the forest and defeated the Naga legions in an epic battle sending them fleeing. In Egypt, Horus a hero who miraculously appeared out of the sky, defeated the Naga forces of chaos under Set and the Scorpion king. These were indeed major setbacks for the Naga, but many people still remained devoted to a version of the rituals honoring the Naga gods. It was in Sumer that a cataclysm evolved from the Naga invasion. Guntur, a human initiate of the Nagas, returned to Tlalocan with the K'ny where he met with the Kepala and plotted their overthrow. At night, he sneaked into the palace and stole Geledek, the spear of power.

Guntur enlisted the aid of the majority of the K'ny, and revolution was brought to the homeland of the Naga Empire. In his homeland, the K'ny were skilled sailors and builders of ships. Guntur brought this technology and expertise with K'ny skilled in these trades of the sea. His knowledge of the sea brought him the respect of the neyalan fisher folk who became his allies. In turn, the Neyalan traded with the Hutan Naga for timber, and they in turn, became allies of Guntur. Together, the trio of Nelayan, Hutan and K'ny under Guntur built a navy of ships and trained sailors contesting the dominion of the northern sea.

The Kepala raised an army of loyal K'ny and Naga to defeat and capture Guntur. Under Raja Gemuk, commander of the K'ny legion, marched to the northern sea to drive Guntur and his traitors into the sea. The Nelayan were out fishing when a storm arose. The sea Dragon attacked the Nelayan with fury. The Nelayan were trapped between Typhoon and Gemuk waiting on the shore when the navy of Guntur arrived with the storm behind the beast. Guntur ordered his crew to release Greek fire into the sea and he let loose arrows of fire to ignite the beast in flames.

As the flames subsided, Guntur ordered his crew to man the oars and attack Typhoon. Weakened and scorched by the fire, Typhoon coughed and choked unable to repel the Nelayan. Guntur hurled the sacred spear Geledek into the side of the sea Dragon. Lightning flashed from the heavens on the seaDragon as he hurled Geledek. Typhoon thrashed the sea into foam as it filled with her blood. As the blood turned the sea red, Typhoon expired and lay down her head. Guntur leaped from his ship onto the back of Typhoon and smashed her head with a mace. He then cut open her belly and entered the inside of the beast. The crew of Nelayan was fearful he might not return. Guntur emerged as he cut the monster in two and severed the head. The fisher folk cheered "Geledek Guntur!" With the raised head of the monster in his hand, Guntur tossed the head into the sea and gathered his forces to meet Gemuk at the shore.

Gemuk and his men witnessed the feat of valor, they were fearful of the might of one who vanquished the goddess of the sea Typhoon. Gemuk saw fear in the eyes of his men. He tried to rally his men, but they turned and ran in fear leaving Gemuk to mount his Dragon to escape.

One of Guntur's men Perkasa drew a dart upon his bow aiming for Gemuk in flight. He let loose the arrow. It shot into the thigh of Gemuk. Another arrow he shot into the belly of the Dragon. The Dragon spun in circles downward with Gemuk holding on as he was hurtling to earth. Gemuk fell off the Dragon as it crashed into a dune near the sea. He staggered off the beast which lay prostrate on the sand. Breaking off the arrow from his thigh, he spit in the sand and took his sword from its scabbard for one last fight. Once he was a mighty warrior, but now he was fat and arrogant. On his breast, he wore the shining Buku takdir, book of the gods. This sacred book was meant to protect its wearer from all ills and opponents. With his sword raised, he yelled out a challenge to Guntur to meet him one on one.

"I avenge TopaNaga!" Gemuk shouted.

Without a word, Guntur strode toward the giant, Gemuk with his blue head crest and shining breastplate. Gemuk's breastplate covered Buku takdir, the sacred texts, for protection in battle. Guntur wore a breastplate of shining obsidian mirror to ward off Gemuk's armor. Gemuk strode to meet him, his gaze upon the human intruder. Within paces of each other, Gemuk whirled his scimitar in a display of prowess. Guntur stood his ground and met his blade with sparks flying. Gemuk broke off and sliced at the head of Guntur. In an instant, Guntur cut off his arm, and the sword fell to earth. Gemuk fell on his knees. Guntur struck his neck and severed his head.

So, Guntur slayed Gemuk, the leader of the Kepala and took Buku takdir.

In his victory, Guntur was wise and knew he needed the defeated Naga to unite both peoples and forge an empire. Queen Wulan was a gentle Naga and consented to bond with Guntur and establish peace between the Nagas and the K'ny. She was a very beautiful Naga woman with exotic features, very wide hips, slim waist, large puffy lips, pointed ears, purple crest over her head, eight large pointed breasts, and silky shimmering skin.

Guntur desired her despite she was a different species. To the surprise of the Nagas and the K'ny she bore him handsome children who had attributes of both parents. His genes were evidently dominant in body physique in various degrees, but their progeny had skin invariably like the Nagas, shimmering with colors as well as a colorful head crest. Wulan was pleased with her children. They were strong and virile like the K'ny, but they could not compute figures as fast as other Naga children. However they far exceeded the Nagas in imagination and creativity.

It was said that the sea dragon Typhoon gave Guntur magic to mate with Queen Wulan. He was thereafter called Suryapurna, son of the Sun. During his reign, the Nagas and K'ny worked together to build an empire that would span the stars. Guntur dreamed of returning to Oceanus and claiming it as his first colony. His rule was known as Jaman Tenang, halcyon days. Guntur was well liked but died before the Nagas returned to Oceanus.

From Wulan sprang a new pantheon of gods to rule Tlalocan and the underworld. Her son Bahadur succeeded his father on the throne. He had a vision of visiting Oceanus like his father, yet he felt no kinship with the humans of Oceanus. He was fond of his K'ny friends though he thought himself superior and elite with his red crest. His younger brother Biru had a blue and green crest. Biru excelled in athletic feats and was very popular. A rivalry developed between the brothers, for Bahadur was jealous of Biru's accomplishments. An expedition to Oceanus was planned and Bahadur as ruler appointed Biru as commander. First, an unmanned probe was sent to a remote region where civilization was just commencing. Bahadur and the elite Kepala wished to assure a profitable colonization.

Before the advent of Aztecs and Mayans on the ocean planet, Biru arrived with his fleet of K'ny and Naga commanders to subdue and indoctrinate the natives with the poisonous weeds of Naga dominion. At the time of the Nagas' arrival in Mesoamerica, the natives were living a somewhat peaceful existence with limited fighting between tribes. Initially, Biru encouraged natives to learn new ways to mine for precious gems, and ores of silver and gold. No Riskani accompanied Biru's command, so they offered no assistance in agriculture or animal husbandry. The natives were frightened at the sight of the K'ny soldiers in their camp. These newcomers were tall and bold with strange weapons but the Naga commander was even taller with a birdlike crest and strange appearance. There was no common language between Naga and native. But the natives treated the Naga as gods and gave them presents to appease them. Soon the Naga were well known throughout the region and could expect homage wherever they went.

Biru made it clear to tribal leaders that the gods were displeased with food offerings only. Lord Biru demanded jewels, gold and silver. Those who resisted Biru sent K'ny to replace the troublemaker with a willing sycophant. Rebellions were met with ruthless bloodshed. Biru told the K'y to learn the native tongue and tell the people that the gods required blood to appease the anger of the gods. Natives were enlisted to build temples to raise their offerings to the stars above the plain of the villagers. K'ny taught young native initiates the rites of priesthood to serve the gods.

Biru's command was very successful in Mesoamerica so he divided his forces to claim new territory. He sent a squadron of ships under Naga Commander Ahumm to Indonesia. It was new territory set apart from the rebellion in the Indian subcontinent. Indonesia was a very successful colony for thousands of years until the coming of Islam. Countless stone temples were erected and the profit in jewels and ore was immense.

Another squadron was sent to Babylon under Naga Cmdr. Barekbaal to instill homage to the new pantheon of gods. The Naga influence in Babylon was epic in proportions in profit and influence lasting until the coming of the Greek invasion of Persia. Another area of influence was the K'ny traders of the Mediterranean. Here K'ny commanders of the Naga were chosen to impress these fledgling sailors and instill in them fear of the gods. A Naga outpost that began in Sumer would branch out to the land of Canaan, Arabia, the shores of the Mediterranean and all its islands. An antediluvian civilization developed that rivaled Egypt in power and glory extending from Canaan, Greece, Italy, and North Africa to Spain. Sea people of this empire explored the Atlantic to the British Isles, down the western coast of Africa even across the Atlantic to Brazil. They did not stop there but traveled through the Red Sea to India and as far as Indonesia. A great cataclysm destroyed their civilization around 1500BC as Thera exploded and sent a Tsunami across Crete and the many islands and coasts of the sea. Survivors revived the culture but it was never as powerful, for Egypt and Greece were on the rise and defeated the sea people. The people of Oceanus proved to be very rebellious and lovers of what they called freedom.

But the most profitable for the Nagas was the rising of civilizations in Mesoamerica. They rivaled the splendor of ancient India and carried on until the coming of conquistadors in 1518 AD. Naga agents infiltrated as far as Peru and established another empire of the Incas for a short time. But this civilization would come to an end with the rise of Christianity and their hatred of the serpent religion. The Mayans were faithful worshippers of the Nagas' serpent religion and adopted a native bird, the Quetzal, to pay homage to the Naga emissary Biru with his iridescent crest of blue and green. Biru was kind to the faithful elite and rewarded them with wealth from the work of the common people. His mission was not of conquest but trade one-sided for the most part.

Biru enjoyed his stay immensely in Mesoamerica, for here he was a god and not just second to the king. Being a hybrid Naga K'ny, he could mate with the humans of Oceanus and maintained a harem of females to generate an elite class among the natives. An interesting note about Naga anatomy: the hybrid males had similar genitalia to their Naga forbearers, a long penis with a spongy horn on the end. This horn received a special organ of the female Naga, a clitoris which could grab the horn and massage the penis to ensure ejaculation. These anatomical features and the recent development of a Naga human hybrid had far reaching developments for a future dynasty of the Naga and their intervention into Oceanus.

Naga males did not enjoy sex with human females as much as with their own kind. However human females sought the Naga hybrid men for they excited them so much more than human men did. It was for this reason that human men began to practice circumcision to mimic the Naga penis with its bulbous horn. The elite Naga hybrid dynasty of Biru continued to foster children from human females to strengthen their bloodline as the Naga line was weakened. Naga hybrid women evolved who also retained Naga genitalia but the cranium was decidedly more human in structure and appearance in most cases. Among these females they did not favor human males unless they were circumcised. When the Naga females did have intercourse with circumcised men they enjoyed it so much more because the human men did not bind and irritate them but continued longer for their sexual pleasure.

As generations of Naga human hybrids progressed, the female progeny exhibited more human physiognomy. Hands and toes reverted from six to five digits, stature was reduced, the forehead became more pronounced as the cerebrum increased in size and the goddess figure emerged. These Naga goddesses had very slim waists, voluptuous breasts, large eyes, wide full lips, long noses, wide hips, large buttocks, and long legs. Similar anatomical features developed in Naga human hybrids for males as well, except the shape of men was less exaggerated but more muscular, strong and tall.

Even those Naga hybrids who did not inherit Biru's genes practiced binding their infant's heads to mimic his sloping forehead. He was very popular with the natives acting as if he was a generous ruler. He showed the priests that even he would bleed to propitiate the gods. After twenty years of adventure and bliss, Biru had to return to Tlalocan and presented his cargo to Raja Bahadur. He left K'ny emissaries to train and hold dominion over the natives. Every century, a starship departed from Oceanus to take its cargo of precious gem, ores and artifacts to the throne of the Kepalain Tlalocan. .

After 1500 years of rule in Mesoamerica the shipments stopped coming to Tlalocan. Shipments were smuggled from China and Indonesia after Islamic takeover in Asia for another hundred years. The Mongol invasion disrupted the last network of Naga shipments with the invasion of Bagdad in 1258 AD. Shipments had been severely curtailed with the rise of Islam centuries before. The Naga elite had grown fat and lazy during the 1500 years of wealth. They were hesitant to send an army to suppress these new cults paying homage to only one god.

Raja Budi, a descendent of Bahadur I, sent a single starship with instructions to K'ny agents to infiltrate these new-found religions and implant the wise serpent knowledge of Naga. These alien incursions occurred just before the 17th Century on approximately 1666 in a distant isle of Indonesia from where it would be disseminated. Evidently, the K'ny agents had been compromised by mating with the natives and assimilated into the population, so new agents were sent in disguise to enter the priesthood of these cults or enter into trader's associations. A century later, another starship was sent with instructions for agents to foment insurrections, promote nihilism and incite wars to produce a state of desolation and chaos thus bringing down native governments.

So, came about the endless wars since that time to the present. Christians and Muslims would preach about a creature and his legions called by various names - Satan, Beelzebub, Lucifer and warn about the wiles of the devil. In modern times the reality of a being such as the 'devil' was thought by many educated people to be a joke and a fairy tale. Little did they know of the reality behind these sermons of preachers. In the wake of world war, communities were ripped apart by war and desolation. Oceanus was vulnerable to invasion.

ABOUT THE AUTHOR

As a naturalist, Jack has hiked extensively in the wilderness of Oregon, Washington, Idaho and California. In his quest to experience nature, he camped under the stars for many nights in the High Desert of the Great Basin, walked under the waterfalls of the Columbia Gorge, viewed the panorama of Dry Falls, bicycled up steep inclines of Sierra Nevada peaks, enjoyed the wonders of Yosemite, Zion, the Sierra Madres of New Mexico, the Grand Canyon, Snake River Valley and Hells Canyon. He currently works as a greenhouse grower sowing seeds for a greener future.

Proof